REVENGING DUNGEON

MONSTER HAVEN BOOK 2

J. D. ASTRA

CHAPTER ONE

HERO FARMING

Hero blood sprayed across the dark walls of the Monster Haven maze beneath the city proper. Greg stepped on the fallen priestess and yanked his hammer from her crushed ribs.

"No time to rest! Get on the next wave," Dolli called from the back of the caster unit. She dropped a Gravity Well just ahead of the frontline heroes as they advanced toward her group of new trainees.

It'd only been a few short weeks since the town of Little Crossroads had become a dungeon, but already Dolli and her remaining monsters were making the most of the dire situation. Heroes—who'd been completely absent when they were a village of citizens—now arrived in droves. They all wanted to see the village turned dungeon and destroy it if they could. But that wasn't in Dolli's agenda; not now, or ever. So, everyone trained in combat, and everyone defended Monster Haven.

Clashes of steel and shouts of combat broke through Dolli's thoughts, returning her to the battle. A dual-wielding fighter crept up at the right flank. Henrietta, the Oakenheart who was *supposed* to be trapping and immobilizing those who broke off from the main group, was too busy sending toxic waves of pollen into the crowd of heroes to notice the danger.

"Watch the right flank!" Dolli called but took no action, knowing that sometimes the best lesson learned was the one directly experienced. She didn't relish it, but sometimes pain was the best teacher.

Henrietta was oblivious to Dolli's warning, grinning and chanting while her thorny vines trapped the heroes. The fighter was nearly upon her.

"Right flank!" Dolli called again. It was too late. The fighter cut down into the Oakenheart's arm, severing her limb at the elbow. Henrietta shrieked and dropped back. Dolli surged forward, protecting the healers in the back from the gap opened in their defenses.

She cast Fold Reality below the attacker, then opened the second portal into the middle of the battle. The hero yelped in surprise at the lack of ground in front of him, then screamed when he fell from the ceiling into stabbing swords and swinging hammers. He was pummeled with more than a little friendly fire.

"Why didn't you help me?" Henrietta screamed and cradled her oozing limb.

Dolli turned, looking past the slender woman to the healer Wispelle. "Get her back out there."

"I'm talking to you!" Henrietta lashed a thorny vine through Dolli's form to get her attention. The pink-and-gold storm of Spark in Dolli's chest swirled with frustration, upsetting and overtaking the midnight blue of her arms and legs.

Dolli looked to the battle. It was well in hand with Greg at the front, so she addressed Henrietta. "I warned you. You knew what you were supposed to be doing—"

"But you let him cut my arm off." She cried through the words, a new Spark-misty forearm growing from the oozing stub that had been left from the fighter's attack.

"No, *you* let him cut your arm off," Dolli corrected. "You were supposed to be watching the right flank, but you were caught up in battle instead of paying attention to your duty."

Henrietta winced and bared her teeth while the arm solidified. It glowed a soft white, and then the rejuvenation spell completed. Her brown- and tan-grained skin was clean and fresh compared to the blood-spattered bicep above it.

"My Spark is low," the Wispelle said and excused himself from the battle. He moved to the back and was replaced with one of the other waiting Wispelle—as Dolli had designed.

The last hero gurgled a final breath and the underground maze of the dungeon fell quiet.

"I don't see why you didn't just help me," Henrietta growled.

Dolli thought on it for a moment, wondering if the truth would incite even more anger from the Oakenheart. "We will all get hurt. We will all die defending our home. We have to get used to it."

Henrietta sneered. "So, you let him cut my arm off so I could *get used to it*?"

"What's all this whinin'?" Greg boomed, pushing through the crowd.

"The negligent witch is back to her lazy ways," Vilhelm—the bear-like Osorath—snarled and stepped up to Henrietta's side to comfort her.

Betrayal prickled the back of Dolli's neck and heat swirled in her stomach. It had only been a few short weeks, not nearly enough time to rid herself of the curse in their tones or the old feelings of resentment.

"And you could do better?" Greg asked Vilhelm.

Vilhelm's lips curled back, revealing sharp teeth. "I wouldn't have trapped us in this tomb, that's for certain. We could be out there taking the fight to the heroes, but instead we're in this dungeon maze, defending what? Flower beds and taverns?"

Julie, the head architect of the whole underground, tutted. "You'd prefer we fought on the streets, in our homes?"

"I'd prefer if we weren't trapped!" Vilhelm's maw snapped in Julie's direction, and Greg prepared for battle.

Dolli put her hand out and shook her head at the massive Blacksmith. The crowd was watching her, Greg, and Julie—they were some of the dungeon's leaders after all—and they couldn't respond to their own people with violence.

"Vilhelm, these dungeon mazes do not just protect flower beds and taverns—or even our homes, Julie. They protect the last bit of our former lives, our passions and pursuits. I wouldn't trade that for taking the fight to the heroes out there. I'm perfectly content with letting the bastards come to us."

"You *would* be content with sitting on your arse," Vilhelm said snidely. Henrietta was quick to laugh in agreement.

"That's enough from the both of ya," Greg said, surprising Dolli. He'd grown more supportive of her leadership since the battle with Keegan, but this was the first time he'd outright defended her.

As much as Dolli appreciated that newfound support, she knew this was *still* the wrong tactic to truly earn their trust. They had to feel heard. That was how everything had worked long ago. She'd listened and made changes.

"You can speak, Vilhelm. I want to hear your grievances."

"I'd have liked it much better if you'd wanted to hear my opinion. I woulda told you how stupid you were to trap us here."

Dolli was losing her patience for his disrespect. "I've heard your complaint. It doesn't change the fact of what we are, a Defender-type dungeon, but it does leave you with an option. You may unbind yourself from this dungeon and leave at any time," Dolli offered the Osorath.

Vilhelm's hackles dropped, his ears smoothing against his head. "That would be suicide."

"It might, but wouldn't you be happier taking the fight to the heroes?" Dolli asked. Her tone was even-keeled, despite the gnawing frustration in her gut. Some of it, she knew, was her *people's* frustration. She felt their thoughts and emotions almost as easily as her own—though she'd grown adept at identifying which was which.

Vilhelm growled. "Why didn't you put it to a vote, let us all decide our fate?"

"We were a mouse fart away from gettin' wiped off the map, lad," Greg said.

A mouse fart was a very small measurement indeed, and an accurate one. If she hadn't made that choice, heroes would've brought in the reinforcements needed to destroy the dungeon core below her cottage, the very thing that sustained their lives and allowed them to respawn.

"Just like she acted when we were dyin' of the plague?" Henrietta sniped.

The growing crowd rumbled with murmurs of agreement and disagreement. Split feelings of injustice and righteousness went to war inside her, neither of which were her own emotions. She'd lived the life of a pariah and accepted her guilt for the lives lost, but she'd also come to terms with the decision. She'd saved more than she'd condemned, and it had been a hard choice to make.

A soft green mist that smelled of morning dew manifested in the room, and all emotion faded. Doubt, worry, fear, everything, all gone. Dolli turned to see Julie, her hands weaving and emanating vibrant light as the spell came to an end.

Julie smiled softly. "There. Now we can think clearly."

"Did you enchant us?" Vilhelm asked, and a pang of anger zipped through the room, inciting the murmurs once more. He must've resisted her spell.

"I just thought it would be easier to talk," Julie said.

"You used your magic against us!" Vilhelm's anger was palpable, riling up the crowd.

"Enough!" Dolli boomed, and a shock wave of power silenced the room.

Dolli closed her eyes. She hadn't meant to use Overlord Presence. She liked to consider herself equal among her people, and that ability was exactly the opposite of equal.

She sighed, and the feeling in the room lightened. "Vilhelm, you are free to do what makes you happy. You as well, Henrietta. But if you stay here, you are committing to being a part of this community. You must defend and protect it. You must do your job, or we could all fail."

Vilhelm stalked away without a word, and half the group disbanded. The remaining monsters looked between one another with confusion, and Dolli waved them off. "There are no imminent threats. Everyone is free to return to their tasks, or whatever you were doing before. We'll train more soon."

Everyone except Greg slipped away into the shadows, heading to the respective postings or exits to get back to the city above.

"That'ns trouble. I know 'cause I was just like him," he warned.

Dolli nodded. "He can stay or leave—or challenge me I suppose, but that wouldn't change the fact that this is a Defender dungeon. We're here for life no matter who is Overlord."

A loud rumbling sound like a volcano preparing to erupt vibrated from Greg's chest. She felt his displeasure, the frustration. He just wanted to get on with his new life. He wanted to craft and make cool traps, fight a few heroes, and enjoy the sunset. So much had been taken from him, and now this was what he had left. He wanted to make the most of it.

Dolli pulled herself from his thoughts. It was strange how deep in their minds she could get when she had them one-on-one. From just a few emotions she could unravel their thoughts, interpret them, almost like telling a story with pictures, but instead it was feelings.

"Well, forge's callin' me," Greg tried to excuse himself.

"Hey, want to blow off a little steam instead?" Dolli asked.

"He's still got that quest, then?"

"I don't know why he won't drop it."

Greg grinned. "Well, let's ask'm."

"Follow me," Dolli said.

She led him up through the dungeon maze to the cottage

where Nubiri had made her roost. It was a tall spire with a platform at the top that supported her egg and had just enough room for Nubiri to curl up with it. Greg had also constructed a bit of metal scaffolding over the cottage that Nubiri could perch on, though she rarely used it. The wyvern perked up when she saw Dolli.

"Ready?" Dolli asked Nubiri with a smile.

"Alwaysss," the wyvern hissed, the desire for vengeance thick in her tone.

Dolli opened the Hero Quest menu. There was Keegan, still holding on to the plague quest. Though Keegan had never returned to Monster Haven of his own volition since the night of his failed guild raid, he just couldn't bring himself to cancel the quest. Dolli didn't understand why.

The "Summon" button wasn't always active, but today it was. Dolli had yet to figure that out, but it didn't matter much. They only summoned him for fun now, and of course to incentivize him to return Nubiri's eggs.

Dolli's thoughts hovered on the summon button. "Three, two, one."

With a blink, she activated the spell to bring the hero across the wide distances of the five kingdoms to her dungeon against his will.

CHAPTER TWO

HORDE ON THE HORIZON

Blinding white summoning light swirled in front of Dolli. Excitement trilled through her, and she closed her menu. She didn't get to kill Keegan often, but she relished it every time.

"I have a fun idea!" she said, putting her hand out to stop Greg and Nubiri from pummeling Keegan the second he materialized.

Dolli cast the first opening for Fold Reality on the ground just in front of the glowing white summoning magic, and the second about ten feet above the first portal. She'd only just figured this trick out with boulders and was excited to try it on a living specimen.

The light coalesced and took shape as the plate-wearing Dusk Knight.

"Again? Have it your way, but I'm not going down without a fight!" Keegan drew his sword and took a step forward. His eyes went wide with fear when his foot fell right into the invisible hole in reality. He dropped from the sky, his hands glowing red. Dolli dodged the incoming Blood Javelin, and Keegan kept falling.

"What is this?" He yelled in confusion. He passed through the folds over and over, picking up speed.

"Think you can hit him?" Dolli asked Greg and Nubiri.

The Bronzite and wyvern exchanged devious smiles.

"Wanna put coin on it?" Greg asked.

"Coin? Ussseless. Battle duty. You take mine, or I take yours," Nubiri offered in exchange, and all the while Keegan picked up speed through the looping portal. Dolli watched the betting with amusement.

"Done," Greg agreed. He stepped up and took a wide stance next to the looping Keegan, gripping his hammer in both hands over his shoulder.

Nubiri stepped to the other side and turned so her side faced the portal.

Keegan screamed endlessly, flailing his arms and legs as he reached out for anything to stop himself. Greg lined up and swung, but missed. Greg cursed and stepped back from the portal. Keegan was just a blur of red, black, and screams plummeting through the loop. If the fold closed, Keegan would smash into the ground, and at those speeds, he'd be jelly in an instant— jelly Dolli didn't want on her newly crafted robes. Dolli backed away to give Nubiri space.

"Running out of time," Dolli warned the wyvern.

"I'll get him," she hissed. Nubiri whipped her tail at the looping Keegan and there was a loud *crack*. Keegan sailed backwards through the street and rolled to a stop fifty feet away, his armor dangling loosely off his chest.

"Ouch," Keegan mouthed breathlessly. His health bar flashed at fifty percent.

"You'll take my duty," Nubiri said to Greg with an impish grin.

"That was pure luck, not skill," the Bronzite said, waving his hammer at her.

Dolli hummed. "Whatever it was, let's finish it."

"Why... are you such... a butthole?" Keegan gasped and pulled his sword from the ground.

"If you'd return Nubiri's eggs, we wouldn't keep summoning

you," Dolli reminded the hero.

Keegan reached out, and ghostly skeleton hands grew from the ground, grasping at Greg. Dolli dropped Gravity Well below Keegan's feet. She followed up by casting Zeal on Nubiri, then conjured a Divine Spark Lance. Being a Dusk Knight meant Keegan was weak to Divine magic, something Dolli had discovered in their previous summonings. It made him *so* much easier to kill.

"Where are the eggs?" Dolli asked again with the force of a Dungeon Overlord.

"Suck my ass," Keegan managed.

Nubiri lunged forward, her bared teeth dripping saliva. Dolli threw the lance, and it slipped past Keegan's dangling chest armor. It speared him all the way through, dropping his health bar to ten percent and throwing him back several feet. Nubiri advanced, pressing her oversized foot against his exposed chest.

Keegan whined. "Okay, I'll tell you."

Dolli held another Divine Spark Lance aimed at his head. "Well?"

Keegan looked up, blood coating his wide grin. "I already sold them at the auction and made a *lot* of money."

"And you call *usss* monsters? You're despicable." Nubiri ended it with a single chomp, decapitating him. The wyvern pulled his head free from his spine and spit it across the road.

"Thanksss for the fun, Overlord," the wyvern said, then retreated to her roost. Dolli could hear the sadness in her voice. Her babies had been *sold*. It infuriated Dolli.

Greg knelt next to the body, rooting through his inventory, Dolli knew. He came away with a few coins and a small ring, and then Keegan's body shimmered into white sparkles. The energy zipped through the sky, off for respawn.

A level-up notification appeared in the corner of Dolli's vision. She opened her menu to find she'd achieved level thirteen and earned two new spells she could allocate points to. She'd used two of her points from levels eleven and twelve into improving her "bread and butter" as Rufus liked to say, Spark Lance and Gravity Well.

She reviewed her upgraded spells one more time.

[Wispelle Ability: SPARK LANCE]

Spell type: Active
Cost: 80 Spark
Cast time: 1.5 seconds
Cooldown: N/A
Duration: N/A
Range: 60 feet
Target: Any
Spark Alignment: Celestial
Description: Fire a lance of pure Spark energy at your target. This energy is neutral.
Effects:

- Spear your target for 2x your Magic Affinity + 2x your Mental Prowess
- Reduce Friendly Fire damage by 25%.
- If your Spark Lance kills the target, absorb 15% of their remaining Spark

Modification: Spend an additional 25 Spark to apply an elemental energy to the Lance.
Disclaimer: Beware of Friendly Fire!

=====

[Wispelle Ability: GRAVITY WELL]

Spell type: Active
Cost: 50 Spark
Cast time: 1.5 seconds

Cooldown: 3 minutes
Duration: 30 seconds
Range: 50 feet
Radius: 15 feet
Target: Area of Effect – Discriminatory
Spark Alignment: Nether
Description: Foes within the field are affected by gravity more severely while friends are less affected.
Effects:

- Foes within the Gravity Well will experience reduced Agility, Stamina, Strength, and Movement Speed by 20%.
- Friends within the Gravity Well will experience increased Agility, Stamina, Strength, and Movement speed by 10%.
- Foes will suffer the debuff "Disoriented" for five seconds when Gravity Well's effects end, causing loss of balance.

=====

The upgrades had done a lot for her; not bad points spent at all.

But now it was time for some new hotness.

[Celestelle Ability: MORTMOSIS]

Spell type: Passive
Spark Alignment: Nether
Description: You feed on death and destruction.
Effects:

- Allow Spark Regeneration while in combat at 5% normal regeneration rate.

- Replenish 1.2 x your Magical Affinity in Spark when an ally dies within twenty feet of you.
- Increase Spark Regeneration by 5% for two minutes when you deal a critical strike to an opponent.
- Gain an additional 1.5 x experience when you deal a killing blow on an opponent.

======

That was an impressive skill, and Dolli could see it helping a great deal with hero farming, but she wasn't going to hastily drop her points without checking the other option—or the other spells she could level up to increase their potency.

[Celestelle Ability: VIRTUOUS LIGHT]

Spell type: Active
Cost: 200 Spark
Cast time: Instant
Cooldown: 2 minutes
Duration: Dependent
Range: 15 Feet
Target: Area of Effect, Cone-shaped
Spark Alignment: Divine
Description: Channel the power of the Sol through your being in a powerful burst.
Effects:

- Any enemy caught directly in the cone will be blinded for 6 seconds and suffer reduced visibility for 30 seconds
- Any enemy within ten feet of the cone will have reduced visibility by 20-50% for ten seconds
- Allies caught within the cone will earn the ZEAL buff for 6 seconds

======

That spell could be another benefit for hero farming, putting Dolli squarely in the middle ranks of combat. But, Mortmosis was more valuable, so the first point went there. Dolli had too few passive abilities, and as tempting as it was to get two brand-new abilities, Dolli had to consider the real purpose of her role in a raid—casting support.

Having the benefit of Spark regeneration while in combat would be crucial to sustained combat. Sometimes the hero waves didn't stop for hours, and the dungeon would suffer deep losses—sometimes even total annihilation. That was weeks ago though. They hadn't all been wiped out for a good six days now—bloody widows must've lost interest in tormenting them for once.

Dolli shook her head. They were well past those horrors now. Onward and upward. She took one last glance at her spell tree.

[Dollitrice Grandmeir – Monster Ability Sheet]

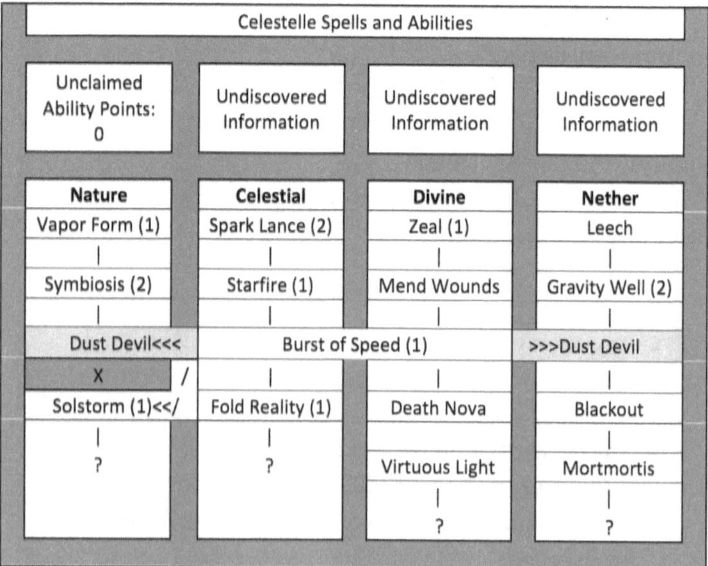

Celestelle Spells and Abilities			
Unclaimed Ability Points: 0	Undiscovered Information	Undiscovered Information	Undiscovered Information
Nature	**Celestial**	**Divine**	**Nether**
Vapor Form (1)	Spark Lance (2)	Zeal (1)	Leech
|	|	|	|
Symbiosis (2)	Starfire (1)	Mend Wounds	Gravity Well (2)
|	|	|	|
Dust Devil<<<	Burst of Speed (1)		>>>Dust Devil
X /	|	|	|
Solstorm (1)<</	Fold Reality (1)	Death Nova	Blackout
|	|		|
?	?	Virtuous Light	Mortmortis
		|	|
		?	?

=====

She looked over her character sheet before closing out of the menus and applied her new stat points, favoring the caster stats, but not skimping on a bit of Constitution.

[Dollitrice Grandmeir – Monster Character Sheet]

Name	Level	Alignment
Dollitrice Grandmeir	**13**	**Celestial**
Creature Type	Experience Points	Affiliation
Celestelle	**155**	**Monster Haven**
Health	Health Regen per sec	Carry Capacity LBS
453	**10.25**	**17.5**
Spark	Spark Regen per sec	Movement Speed Bonus
1014	**27.05**	**15%**
Agility	Constitution	Magical Affinity
11	**19**	**52**
Mental Prowess	Stamina	Strength
41	**17**	**5**
Melee Damage per sec	Ranged Damage per sec	Spell Damage
9.9	**21.7**	**81.0**
Crit Chance	Dodge Chance	Spell Crit Chance
6.00%	**9.90%**	**29.67%**
Armor Rating	Armor Piercing	Celestial Res.
12.00%	**8.00%**	**28.67%**
Divine Res.	Nature Res.	Nether Res.
34.13%	**23.21%**	**27.30%**

=====

Dolli felt the drag of exhaustion pulling on her limbs. She was getting close to hitting her bedtime. "I need to do a few things before I go to the Lifewell. Do you need anything from me?" she asked Greg, who appeared to be lost in his menus as well.

Greg's pitch-black eyes focused on her. "Nothin' at all. I'll keep things going down in the fighting pits while you rest."

Dolli nodded and waved farewell. Training the troops was a necessary part of being Overlord, but by Nevheröld did it take up a lot of her time. The dungeon was creeping up on Level 6, and Dolli was praying for some kind of "Combat Leader" role she could pass off—perhaps to Brene, the ex-soldier. She knew this was wishful thinking, and she had other matters to attend to: potion creation.

She made her way over to the creators' district, where the old, abandoned buildings were being renovated into profession and crafter houses. Dolli herself had moved much of her materials from her cottage to a new alchemy lab she'd created near Greg's smithy.

With the Health and Spark potion reserves low, Dolli knew that was her priority. All the dungeon pits had "refill" stations available to the dungeonfolk who were battling heroes, and though they needed less filling recently, it was still necessary. Health and Spark regeneration potions were not complex, and she found the work relaxing, almost meditative.

When she'd made a few good batches and corked the kegs in their respective storage areas, she decided it was time to get to bed. She passed several different bands of monsters on her way to her seat of power and the place where all things in the dungeon were made possible. Since controlling the seat of power was essential for respawning her monsters—and herself—she had it under round-the-clock observation. It was supposed to be Nubiri's watch, and Dolli was surprised the wyvern wasn't there. Though Greg had agreed to take her battle duty that night, that didn't absolve her of her watch until then.

Moreover, Nubiri didn't leave her unhatched child unattended, so Dolli opened her menu and sent a message to the Guardian through the Overlord system: *What's going on? Where are you?*

Dolli panned to the Lifewell. There were a few monsters doing their time to ward off the exhaustion debuff, but Nubiri wasn't among them—so she wasn't dead.

The clouds above swirled with the twisting of air, and Nubiri dropped through them like a meteor. She tucked her wings and twirled, playing on the air current. That was when Dolli saw it: something clutched in Nubiri's right claw. There were flailing arms and legs poking out from under Nubiri's grasp, and Dolli heard the panicked screams of something dog-like.

The huntress unfurled her wings just before impact with the city and pulled up, but not before slamming the creature in her claws to the cobblestones at Dolli's feet. The monster had long fluffy ears the color of mud, a pink snout at the end of a short maw, and black circles in the fur around its eyes. It rolled to the side and coughed up blood, its health bar flashing at critical low.

On instinct, Dolli dropped beside the creature and held a minor rejuvenation potion to its lips.

Nubiri snarled and landed on her perch. "This creature is of the Horde."

Dolli scowled, then poured just a bit of the potion into the monster's mouth. It coughed and sputtered, then opened big brown eyes to look at Dolli.

Its pupils dilated, then shrank, and the creature recoiled. "Why you do this?"

"You were dying, and I didn't know if you had a dungeon. Are you free-roaming?" Dolli asked in a calm, soothing voice.

"I told you already, it's of the Horde," Nubiri said again with more force.

Those words meant nothing to Dolli, but she assumed the Horde was a dungeon. Well, better to have been safe than sorry. "What are you doing in my zone?"

"I—I came to look, sniff, learn." The creature pulled its furry feet under it, protecting its belly.

Nubiri climbed down the rungs of her perch and stood before the monster, blocking its view of her egg. "It's a scout. It came too close to the village, on its way back to its Overlord—"

"Must do this! He will eat my *yekipyip*!" the beast snapped back defensively. The hair on its back rose, and its lips curled up to the pink nose, exposing silvery teeth like razors.

The word it had said, *yekipyip*, was spoken with a dog-like bark, its native tongue mayhap. Whatever it meant, the thing was spooked half to death, and not of Dolli or Nubiri.

"You cannot let it return," Nubiri warned.

Dolli took a deep breath. "There's nothing we can do to prevent that. Overlords can recall their monsters when they're not in combat."

"We keep it hurting, but not dead, and it cannot return," Nubiri said with a vicious snarl, and Dolli questioned for a fraction of a second whether she'd selected the right monster for the role of Guardian.

Nubiri was trying to protect the village—probably her unhatched egg more. But she had developed an affinity for the dungeon, especially for the freedom and protection she was afforded, not to mention egg sitting, so Nubiri was simply doing her job and Dolli didn't understand.

"What's this Horde?" she asked the wyvern.

Nubiri's tongue shot out with a hiss. "Monsters killing monsters. He roams the land, taking the weak and crushing the powerful—never more powerful than himself..." The wyvern dipped her head solemnly. "He stole our roost."

Dolli nodded. She understood Nubiri's hatred of the creature better now. It represented the thing that led to the untimely death of her mate and the theft of two of her eggs.

But that didn't mean Dolli was going to torture this creature. It wasn't at fault for what happened to Nubiri's mate or eggs. It likely wasn't responsible for anything other than ensuring its own survival.

"How do you know it's of this Horde?" Dolli asked Nubiri.

The wyvern's nostrils flared. "I smell the reek of Kelzoul, its Overlord."

Dolli's brow furrowed. She had to take Nubiri on her word that she *smelled* the essence of the other monster in it. She trusted the wyvern, but to torture this creature over that? She couldn't do it. There had to be another way.

"We're not going to hurt you," Dolli said.

The foxy creature cocked its head, puzzled.

Nubiri growled. "You would let it bring ruin to your home? Have you not made this mistake before?"

Dolli glared at the wyvern. She'd have to talk with whoever was giving Nubiri unnecessary history lessons. "I've got this."

Dolli looked back to the scout. "We can kill you and send you back to your Overlord, but I have a feeling you don't want that. Join us instead. We'll keep you safe and give you a community to thrive in."

The beast cowered and backed away, panic setting in. "Can no do. He come and find and eat all *yekipyip*."

Dolli spoke in a hushed tone. "What's your name?"

"Bakreh. Can no stay. Let go, or let die."

"I won't let him escape," Nubiri said with a snarl. "He will bring back destruction."

"What's going on here?" Rufus, Dolli's Lieutenant, asked with a scowl. Aside from running things in Dolli's downtime, Rufus had appointed himself head of immigration. Every new monster came through him for orientation and instructions.

"This creature is a scout for murderersss. We must detain it." Nubiri lowered her head and bared her teeth.

Bakreh's hackles shot straight up and he curled his back to look larger. He was only about forty pounds, and no bigger than a cattle dog, but boy did he put on a show for survival.

Dolli put herself between the wyvern and Bakreh. "We won't do that. We mustn't fall so low."

"Your righteoussssness is misguided. This creature is a murderer, just like its Overlord."

"No, it isn't," Dolli declared. "He's just a scout, and he's scared. He doesn't want to go back to Kelzoul. We must help him."

Bakreh whimpered. "No matter. He comes. We knew you here

already. I came to sniff, see level, see size and number. Tell how many hordlings to bring."

"But if you stay, he won't know any of those things. Maybe he'll think we're too powerful, like Nubiri said, and he won't come near," Dolli offered.

"No work. No work!" Bakreh said, shaking his head and trembling. "He come!"

Bakreh darted for the edge of the nearest alley, but Nubiri was already on him. Her teeth snapped down around his legs before Dolli could stop her. Nubiri ripped Bakreh side to side, then tossed him into the air like a rag doll.

This was not going how Dolli had planned.

CHAPTER THREE

WOLFKIN'S WARNING

The beast hung in midair, giving Dolli a second to react. She cast Fold Reality below him and opened the second portal behind her. Bakreh came down with a bone-shattering crack and a yelp. Nubiri's too-large snout smashed into the cobblestones instead of passing through the portal—something Dolli had learned in her practice with boulders. There was some kind of mass restriction at this level, and if a creature or object exceeded that limit, it wouldn't interact with the portal. Good news for Bakreh, not so great for Nubiri.

Dolli dropped to the wolfkin's side. His health was below ten percent and dropping. Blood matted the fur on his chin, smearing against Dolli's half-corporeal hand as she put the health potion to his lips. Bakreh pulled away, clenching his jaw so tight that Dolli couldn't get the mouth of the bottle between his sharp teeth.

"Don't do this. Let us help you," Dolli pleaded.

"No can help. He come for all *yekipyip*. But…" Bakreh coughed up more blood. "You give yours, he let others go. Could work. My Overlord do this…" His eyes were glossy, and his health hovered at 1%.

"Don't let it die!" Nubiri roared.

Dolli couldn't keep the creature here, she couldn't torment it the way Nubiri had asked. With a gurgle, Bakreh went limp in her misty arms.

"Fool! He'll bring them to us!" Nubiri stomped around in a fury.

"Bring who?" Boji, Monster Haven's very first recruit, asked from the gathering crowd.

Dolli stood as the wolfkin Bakreh disappeared in a shower of orange sparks and floated southeast. "This *Horde*. A dungeon that hunts other dungeons. But they were already coming—that creature's report will do little to change that."

Nubiri snorted. "If you'd kept it alive…"

"What would it have bought us?" Dolli snapped. The exhaustion debuff was close at hand, and she was feeling the negative effects on her calm. "I would've tortured him for what, a few extra hours? That's not who we are."

"Overlord is right. We hurt heroes, not our own," said Boji.

"But if they're going to murder us, doesn't that change things a bit?" Henrietta asked.

The group was growing by the minute. Dolli decided to stop rumors in their tracks and tell everyone what was going on. She opened her Overlord menu and started a new dungeon-wide message: *There is an enemy dungeon to the southeast that may be planning to attack and destroy us.*

She paused, looking to her people. Chances were slim that negotiation would work, but Dolli had a secret bargaining tool. She could summon heroes. If she promised this Horde a portion of the kills and loot, perhaps that would appease them. The other options were far grimmer, and not something she wanted to consider before diplomacy was completely off the table.

I will travel to their camp and attempt to negotiate a truce. If that fails, I'll return, and we'll discuss the next step.

"Negotiate? Truce? What are these words?" Nubiri asked.

Nubiri was so well-spoken, Dolli was surprised she didn't know. But these weren't words she required in her vocabulary as a wyvern. "I'm going to ask them not to hurt us in exchange for a portion of our summoned heroes."

Nubiri barked a laugh. "You would sooner move Sol from the sky than Kelzoul with such tactics. He does not negotiate, or truce. He will take what he wants, destroy the rest, and move on. I know this. Our roost was ten mated pairs strong, and he took everything from us. His army never ended."

"Well, I'm guessing you didn't offer him a deal as sweet as I will," Dolli said with a cocky smile that belied her anxiety.

"Send me, Overlord," Rufus offered.

Dolli shook her head. "No, I think this is one of those things I need to take care of myself. I will need to prove my claim."

Like a punch to the gut, the exhausted debuff slammed into Dolli. She drooped to the ground and groaned at the pop-up in her vision.

[Debuff: Exhausted]

All stats reduced by 25%. Movement speed reduced by 50%. Spark and Health Regeneration reduced by 75%. Damage dealt to you is doubled. Damage you deal is halved.

Effects are amplified by 2x in 3:59:50.

=====

"You need to rest. Please, send me," Rufus offered again.

Dolli checked the Lifewell. Only two monsters were on respawn, so if she diverted the other four Lifestream slots to herself, she could regenerate four times as fast, making it only an hour of downtime. That shouldn't be so long that the Horde could sneak up on them. No, if Dolli was understanding Nubiri right, their coming would be obvious for miles and days.

Dolli picked herself up. "I'm going to expedite my rest, but before I go, we need to start working on fortifications—just in case."

Since coming into a comfortable cadence of murdering heroes, the round-the-clock work of improving the dungeon had slowed to allow the dungeonfolk downtime to relax and enjoy the hobbies of their previous lives, or new ones altogether. Dolli wished now she'd pushed them harder, but that was a fruitless thought.

"Rufus, get everyone who's awake tasked with wall improvements, and we need Julie strategizing on how best to handle an endless army marching through our maze. Get Greg up here working on any armor and weapon improvements we can manage."

The crowd had come alive with chatter about the situation, many people talking with Nubiri about her knowledge—Henrietta and Vilhelm among them.

Dolli sighed. "I'm sorry to leave you like this, but please field the questions of the dungeonfolk about this situation. Let them know I am handling it personally and that everything is going to be okay."

Rufus lowered his voice and said, "Is it?"

"That remains to be seen. At best, we may forge a tenuous alliance with dungeon murderers, at worst we'll be at war."

"Nubiri," Dolli said louder, getting the wyvern's attention. "The wolfkin creature, he said Kelzoul would eat our 'yekipyip.' Do you know what that means?"

Nubiri snorted, curls of green smoke leaking from her flared nostrils. "I don't know that word, but I know what he meant. The *sjæl*, what allows us to bind to a seat of power, and roost. The gold that was inside me that changed green when I joined you. The orange that was the wolfkin when he returned to his master. The white that is the dead heroes. You understand me?"

Dolli nodded. "I believe I do."

Respawning was not a foreign concept, though they'd only become capable of it recently. While their deaths were sometimes traumatic, coming back was a lot nicer than staying dead. Dolli didn't want to take that away from any of her people.

She didn't want to lose it either.

"I must rest now," Dolli said to Rufus, who nodded then turned to the crowd.

He lifted to his full height of nine feet and spoke loudly. "Everyone, come to me for new assignments."

Dolli opened the Overlord menu and updated the settings, redirecting the open Lifestream slots to herself, then selected the "Recall" button. The sunset world dissolved in a burst of green sparks, then returned a fraction later to the darkness of twilight. An hour and fifteen minutes had passed for Dolli in the blink of an eye.

To her relief, her exhaustion debuff was gone, so she got to work. All the dungeonfolk had been assigned tasks to fortify the dungeon, which had leveled up to six while she was gone.

[Congratulations – Your dungeon has reached Level 6]

Unused Monster Slots: [5/200]
Undistributed Roles: [1/6]
Open Lifestream Slots: [4/6]
Unclaimed Overlord Ability Points: [2]
[4] levels remain until next dungeon ability: Modulate; Resolve.

=====

Dolli focused on the two new dungeon abilities until their information came into view.

[Dungeon Ability: Modulate]

Transform your dungeon to respond to a threat once every [7] days. Transformation is permanent until Modulate is used again. Transformation is dependent on the enemy threat level: Miniscule, Moderate, Extreme, Legendary.

Dungeon will rearrange itself automatically in [60 seconds] to best fight the assessed threat.

======

[Dungeon Ability: Resolve]

Strengthen the dungeon and its monsters once a day for [.5] hours. Dungeon monsters will have all stats increased by 100%. Dungeon traps will restore to full durability unless they are disabled or destroyed. Damage to dungeon buildings, passages, temples, or treasuries will be repaired automatically over [.5] hours.

======

The Resolve ability was undeniably the best option. It would make fighting heroes a cinch—well, for half an hour at least. Dolli assumed because that number was enclosed in brackets that it was something she could affect or improve upon. That would be an even bigger boon in the future.

She couldn't just disregard Modulate, though. The more the dungeon grew, the harder it was for Julie to keep up with all the modifications. Heroes learned their patterns after a few days, and Julie was almost constantly making updates to one floor or another. The time restriction on that was also bracketed, denoting possible improvements. Dolli knew that once the dungeon was at level twelve or greater, it would be nearly impossible to keep it fresh regularly. And since the ability would automatically respond to whatever threat was thrown at them, they wouldn't have to make that judgement themselves, saving hours of thought.

Indeed, they were both powerful. She would have to put it to a vote, but she was leaning toward Modulate, since it was the right long-term option.

She spent a quick moment going through the Overlord Abilities. The first was an updated Chat system. She could target specific groups instead of blasting the entire dungeon or area around her every time she wanted to deliver a message, which would be incredibly useful. Not only that, but her officers could use the chat with her.

While Nubiri wouldn't ever have any apprentices, Greg, Julie, and Dolli could all take on two or more as they leveled up. Being able to talk to one another while miles apart was the kind of Hero Magic Dolli didn't understand but wasn't going to turn down. It reminded her of the Vital Line ability she'd once had as a Regnant, but that was for direct communication with other Regnants. It'd made the difference for effective containment of the plague, and Dolli was certain the dungeon chat ability would be just as useful in saving their skins now as monsters.

Dolli didn't have any more time to waste if she was going to get ahead of this and maybe save her people. She selected the upgraded Chat ability and then moved on to the next. There were two more staring her down: Lifewell Upgrade and Multitasking.

Dolli had already used the Lifewell upgrade once, and it was powerful, but the Multitasking ability would allow her to have only half of her vision taken up by a screen, meaning she could watch two different ones at once—the map and the chat for example—or she could watch one and her surroundings. It sounded like a useful upgrade that she'd end up getting eventually, so she decided to go for it now.

When she'd finished the Overlord ability selection, she was bombarded by another pop-up for leveling up to fourteen. Dolli growled and went through the motions.

The level didn't come with any new abilities, and there wasn't anything she was hankering for, so she saved the ability point and quickly assigned her stat points: two for Mental Prowess, two for Magic Affinity, and one for Constitution. Slowly, very slowly, she was becoming harder to kill, but she was still very much a glass cannon.

[Dollitrice Grandmeir – Monster Character Sheet]

Name	Level	Alignment
Dollitrice Grandmeir	**14**	**Celestial**
Creature Type	Experience Points	Affiliation
Celestelle	**89**	**Monster Haven**
Health	Health Regen per sec	Carry Capacity LBS
500	**10.44**	**18**
Spark	Spark Regen per sec	Movement Speed Bonus
1112	**28.50**	**14%**
Agility	Constitution	Magical Affinity
11	**20**	**54**
Mental Prowess	Stamina	Strength
43	**17**	**5**
Melee Damage per sec	Ranged Damage per sec	Spell Damage
10.3	**22.6**	**88.2**
Crit Chance	Dodge Chance	Spell Crit Chance
6.25%	**10.31%**	**30.97%**
Armor Rating	Armor Piercing	Celestial Res.
12.50%	**8.00%**	**29.82%**
Divine Res.	Nature Res.	Nether Res.
35.50%	**24.14%**	**28.40%**

=====

With that done, she held her breath as she closed the menu for, hopefully, the final time. No new pop-up appeared, and she was left in the sitting room of her cottage, alone. She looked to her rocking chair, the low-burning embers in the fireplace, and the old tea on the table. It was home, but it felt cold despite the glowing hearth.

What Bakreh had said before he died drifted through Dolli's thoughts. If she sacrificed herself, the others could be saved. Was he telling the truth or just trying to convince her to make it easy for them to sweep in and annihilate everything?

She had to keep her mind on the task at hand. She wasn't ready to roll over and die just yet. Maybe twenty wyverns couldn't hold off the Horde, but Monster Haven had grown into a formidable dungeon over the past few weeks. It was possible they could fight Kelzoul back and make him move on. Nubiri said he would never take on something more powerful than he was...

But was that just delaying the inevitable? He would move on, destroy smaller dungeons, then return for Monster Haven. Dolli only saw two horrible futures: eternal war or the void of death.

Unless her negotiations worked. She could lure Kelzoul into a comfortable lull, gaining power and converting his monsters all the while, until he was weak enough to destroy. That was the only way the dungeons of Hafheim would ever be safe.

But if her negotiations didn't work, they would need a backup plan to protect themselves. Dolli went back into the Overlord menu and panned to the Dungeon Abilities. On the right side was the Officers and Roles section, which had just one role unallocated. There were a few options still open, but she'd been eyeing one since level five when the recruited goblins had truly proven themselves masters of weapon modification: Tinkerer.

It was a type of engineer role that focused specifically on the generation of plans. A Tinkerer could create new designs for traps, weapons, building upgrades, and so much more. It was an important role she probably should've given out sooner... but there was no time like the present.

She opened her chat: *Boji, Deetu, would you come to the cottage?*

She only had to wait a moment before the two were knocking on her door. She showed them in, and they took a seat at her table. Dolli used her new multitasking ability to keep just the Officers and Roles panel open while she watched the goblins. Deetu was still quite small and nimble while Boji had grown to be nearly five and a half feet tall. He was much more muscular, and Dolli assumed he'd been putting a lot of his points into Strength.

"I called you here because there's a role I need filled. Boji, you have shown great aptitude for creativity, and Deetu, you're already a skilled engineer. The role I have is called Tinkerer, and I wanted to offer it to one of you. The role would have you discovering new plans to help keep the dungeon protected and upgraded."

Boji's eyes lit up at Dolli's description of the role.

"You can only give it to one, right?" Deetu asked.

"That's right. I wanted you to be able to decide who wanted it more. It would be a lot of hard work, and you'd have to reduce your fighting rotation to accommodate it. It comes with responsibility, too, like attending the daily meetings."

Deetu looked to Boji. "I've had enough crafting to fill a lifetime. I want to relax."

Boji grinned. "I love this role. I accept it. I will work very hard."

Dolli nodded. "I know you will. You may want to consider diverting some of your stat points toward Mental Prowess, as I think it's an important factor in the role."

Boji nodded vigorously. "All the points for Mental Prowess from now on."

Dolli laughed. "I don't think you need to be *that* extreme, but it might be a good idea to put most of them there, at least for a time."

Dolli pulled the pin from the ether and held it out to Boji. He grabbed it delicately with his thick fingers and smiled wider. "I'm so happy."

[Boji of Haven has accepted the role of Tinkerer!]

A Tinkerer can deconstruct and reverse engineer many different workings of science. They can combine ideas to make new inventions or upgrade existing inventions. The Tinkerer gets a passive bonus to Mental Prowess 1.2 x Role Level. Current bonus for Boji of Monster Haven: +9 Mental Prowess.

The Tinkerer may take on one apprentice at level [5] and a second at level [10]. The Tinkerer will gain new abilities at levels [3], [6], [12], [24], [42], and [60].

======

"Good," Dolli said. "I need you starting on weapon upgrades right away. If things don't go as I hope with the Horde, we will need a good offense."

"I will do the best job, I promise!" Boji said and moved toward the door. "Starting right now!"

Deetu waved and followed Boji out the door with a grin, leaving Dolli alone in the cabin again. She took a deep breath and focused on what was next: alchemy time.

She moved over to the renovated alchemy lab. Thanks to the new technologies supplied by the goblin crews, her shop was even better than it had been before the plague. They'd been able to salvage some of the zeppelin wreckage and repurpose it into functional burners Dolli could utilize for smaller batches of potions.

Which was exactly what Dolli needed now. There were just enough pelimint leaves for two more Spark potions. Dolli had a sneaking feeling she would need all the help she could get if things went wrong in negotiations. She got to work brewing the leaves in water not brought to a boil, but close. Purple steam rose from the small pot. In a matter of minutes, the green-and-silver tea would be ready for bottling with a sephrim seed, which would dissolve in the acidic fluid to create the potion.

While she waited, she ground up five ogre beans—aptly named for their enormous size and reddish pigment. She mixed the pink powder with boiling water until she had a thick soup in her massive cauldron. She pulled the lever next to her workbench to operate the mechanical arm that moved the iron pot from the fire to a basin of cool water.

The arm slowly lowered the pot into the water. The metal of the cauldron whined and steam hissed as the pot and its contents rapidly cooled. Dolli approached when the bubbling water quieted, then dripped oil of moonsylph into the ogre bean brew.

It was one of the rarer potions, despite both ingredients being plentiful. The process was hard to get right. It had to be well timed, and the right temperature. Most potions weren't terribly harmful when done incorrectly—most.

She finished off the two Spark Regen potions, then stored them in her inventory. The Constitution potion, a clear, pinkish color the thickness of honey, she mixed slowly with more cold water, thinning it out and changing the color to a deeper, sunset color.

With the potion complete, Dolli funneled the mixture into several large kegs set up next to the cauldron. Now anyone could come refill their healing potions whenever they needed, as long as they didn't break their bottles—which happened far too often. One of Greg's apprentices had learned to blow glass, but his bottles were still useless.

Dolli corked the last keg with the automated hammer when the door to her shop opened and Greg squeezed inside. He had to duck to fit through the opening.

"I was able to make you upgraded Spark Channelers," he said, wasting no time with pleasantries. He pulled the new equipment from thin air, manifesting it from his inventory.

The silver bands were carved with intricate swirls, half-moons, and radiant starbursts—though the second one looked as if the bottom half was unfinished. Dolli accepted the gift and looked at the information sheet.

[Celestial Spark Channelers of Mental Prowess]

Armor Type: Jewelry
Class: Rare—Expert Forged
Spark Alignment: Celestial
Effects:

- +24 Mental Prowess
- +12 Magical Affinity
- Decrease Spark costs for Celestial aligned spells by 25%
- Increase Spark costs for Nature aligned spells by 10%

Celestial Sol flows through your being, banishing the dark.

======

Greg cleared his throat. "I didn't getta finish the designs, so I'll need 'em back when you return."

"I'm grateful. These will surely be helpful if our chat doesn't go well."

"About that," Greg started, shifting his weight from side to side. "Well, good luck."

Dolli felt he had more to say, but that was his business to tell her or not. "Thank you."

Greg nodded, then left. Strange man. He wanted to kill her for the throne for years, then suddenly he was worried about her. Or maybe he was worried about her ability to negotiate. Either way, he wished her well on her journey and it was a significant improvement from their past interactions.

Dolli packed up a few health potions for herself, then double-checked all her gear. She was ready to go. But was she ready to face a murderer and broker a deal to save her dungeon?

Whatever it took, she'd keep them safe.

CHAPTER FOUR

AIRTIGHT

Dolli floated through the darkening forest, unconcerned with what could be lurking beyond the light cast by her glowing body. In fact, Dolli was wishing she'd encounter some of the Horde's scouts so she could better find their camp! She'd been wandering for twelve hours in the heat of the sun, and didn't know if she was any closer. If only she had some of her Wilds magic back, she'd use the Wayfinder spell that very instant.

Dolli looked to the sky, confirming the position of the South Saber Constellation to ensure she was still headed in the right direction. She was, so she diverted her attention back to her speech, the moving statement she would say to Kelzoul to prevent the annihilation of her home.

"Strike a bargain. Heroes to farm, loot and riches. Twenty percent to start, with a section of the tower all to yourselves." She mumbled the highlights, confirming that the deal sounded plenty enticing.

Gods, what kind of mess was she getting herself into? If only that damn Hero Magic had picked Greg as the Regnant of Little Crossroads. They'd probably still be a village! But then, Kelzoul would still be coming—and the citizens wouldn't have the ability to respawn. They'd be at the mercy of heroes coming to their aid, and Dolli knew all too well how reliable that was.

Dolli stopped, frustrated. She could just recall herself to the Lifewell, call it a day, say that she tried but couldn't find them. Plus, she'd said she would return within a day. At this rate, that wasn't going to be possible. If she went home, maybe she could find a potion in her book that might help guide the way.

Yes, there was still some of Bakreh's blood on the stones outside her hut. She could mix it with a tracking potion and that would surely do the trick. Dolli opened her Overlord menu, but stopped when she heard the crack of a branch.

She whirled, looking toward the sound, and dimmed the light of her glowing body to avoid detection. The wind rustled through the trees and crickets hummed, but nothing moved. She turned again, looking all around. There... a rope hidden among the leaves of a tree.

It wasn't a highly sophisticated trap. Dolli saw the bent branch far above rigged to snap out at the slightest touch and yank unsuspecting victims from the ground. Well, luckily for Dolli, no noose could hold her.

She took it as a sign she was on the right track and kept moving.

"Gotcha," was the last word Dolli heard before an oversized glass jar dropped from the canopy and slammed into the dirt around her.

Two creatures, not dissimilar to Bakreh, appeared from stealth in the brush beside her and put their claw-tipped paws against the glass. They turned it once, twice, and at the third there was a *pop* as the air compressed around Dolli.

She looked down as the evolved wolfkin creatures lifted the jar. The dirt, leaves, and grass that had been below were now trapped in the three-foot-tall jar with Dolli. She probed the bottom with a hand, seeing if she could detect a gap where she could slip some of her Spark through, but there wasn't one. So, it was airtight. An interesting feat of engineering for certain, though it

seemed to have limited potential for trapping things other than…
Wispelle.

The jar was designed to trap creatures like Dolli. This jar was probably *specifically* for trapping Dolli, because Bakreh told Kelzoul everything. No matter.

She looked out at her captors, barely able to hear the low growls exchanged between the wolfkin. A taller, more humanoid creature with skin the color of an orange creamsicle and beefy arms barked commands at the wolfkin. They wrapped straps over the top of Dolli's jar, then down around the bottom like a sling. The bigger wolfkin pulled the straps tight across his shoulders and stomach, then dropped to all fours.

The dirt came piling down on top of Dolli, and she coughed. She smacked against the left side of the tube, then the right, left, back, until she pressed her hands against the sides to stabilize with the jar. The wolfkin was running at a good speed in near total darkness, so it must've had some killer night vision.

Even if all of the Horde's monsters were as fast as this creature —which she doubted—it would take them at least as long to reach Monster Haven as it had taken Dolli to reach them. But they wouldn't be that fast.

They would need the equipment to make potions, repair weapons, and the like near the battlefield, or near enough that it wouldn't take too long to retreat to. Kelzoul would be ruthless and efficient, keeping the spawn point and the battle reinforcements nearby. Twelve hours was much too far away, so they'd have to be looking for another location to settle before beginning their assault.

Dolli would need a good look at their camp to figure out just how much they'd have to move. Given the firelight peeking through the trees, she assumed that was just around the corner. She hadn't been able to detect the wolfkin in stealth, which meant they were a few levels higher than her. What if all the creatures were higher than her?

Her captor slowed to a trot as he breached the tree line to a field of stumps. Ironworks smoked, and the ring of hammers on anvils reverberated through Dolli's glass prison. There were at least five smithies she could see, with emaciated goblins working the bellows.

They moved through the smoggy blacksmith section to a row of grinding wheels. White sparks flicked off the edges of fresh-forged swords that stocky humanoids pressed to the rotating stones. Dolli took quick count of them all and filed the information away for her analysis. There were at least ten heavy stones. They'd likely bring only a few to the front at first and bring the rest in later as time and need demanded.

They reached a sort of barracks where long tarps covered recently crafted tent frames. Inside were row upon row of triple-stacked hammocks, some full of slumbering creatures. Dolli assumed based on the dryness of the wood that they'd been there at least a few weeks—perhaps even before Little Crossroads had been turned into a dungeon.

Dolli didn't want to think about what could've happened had the Horde rolled through the failing village of citizens. They all would've been dead in a matter of hours, with no chance of respawn.

The closer they came to the center of camp, the larger and more detailed the tents became. Some were kitchens with massive bubbling pots full of a thick brown stew and kegs lined up on every table. They were packed with monsters. She was stunned by their diversity. She'd seen at least twelve distinctly different species upon her arrival, while her dungeon had only four.

The creatures scooped the brown mush out of shallow bowls with hunks of bread, some casting brief glances up at Dolli. In the eyes of some she saw malice and pleasure, but in others she saw sad detachment. To them, Dolli was just another victim they couldn't care about.

Sleeping tents and kitchens, two things Dolli's dungeon didn't have to worry about. Her monsters had to return to the Lifewell every twenty-four hours, but had no requirements to eat or sleep.

Perhaps because the wandering dungeon was always on the move, there was no time to tap into Hafheim and find a Lifestream. Or maybe it was some other requirement. Either way, it was required, and that made them weak.

The Horde troops would be on meal and sleep rotations, so there would be even more equipment to move, as well as troops being sent to hunt and gather for their meals. This would make them vulnerable to many kinds of sabotage.

The tents were becoming even more extravagant as they went on, and the spaces between them greater. This must be where the officers stayed, which meant Dolli was likely not far from the Overlord himself, Kelzoul.

Finally, they approached a wooden gate guarded by two of the tall, beefy bipedal creatures with coral-colored skin that swirled with patches of white. They wore brightly colored, advanced looking armor of reds, purples, blues, greens, and whites. They certainly stuck out in the camp as the favored people.

To the left of the gate was a small hut marked by a screaming face, covered in blood, with long silver hair. It was menacing, a warning. *Don't you dare open this door*, the blood drawing said.

The wolfkin slowed to a stop, then stood upright as he approached the guards at the gate. Dolli waved the dust particles away and pressed her hands to the glass, trying to detect their words. They weren't speaking the common tongue, that was for sure, but whatever they were saying, they were happy about it.

One of the guards took off at a jog, and the other opened the gate, waving the wolfkin inside with a grin. The other side of the wood-pike wall was a horror of cruelty unlike anything Dolli had ever seen.

Spiked whips, knives large and small, fire tongs, pokers, tweezers, needles, and all manner of objects that had no proper business being next to one another lined the walls. Tables with straps to hold down victims were stained red with blood. Chains with massive hooks on the end dangled from hastily crafted suspension contraptions.

The wolfkin marched through puddles of fetid blood and chunks of flesh to a tall building crafted of wood, straw, mud, and cloth. Smoke rose from the triangular top, where a hole had been cut in the canvas serving as a roof to let the heat of a fire out.

This was it. Time to strike a deal with a real monster.

CHAPTER FIVE

KELZOUL'S PROMISE

The wolfkin stopped at the flap of the Overlord's tent and announced his presence. The flap pulled away, revealing a dark hut lit by a large fire at the center. Dolli could barely see around the sides of the wolfkin's head, but took note of three, even larger, coral-skinned creatures gathered around the fire. The wolfkin's head blocked Dolli's view of what they were all looking at.

The walls were adorned with weapons and armor, show things of conquered heroes—or perhaps dungeons. A ring of wooden benches surrounded the fire, where a rotating wild boar grew pink and crispy. Such extravagance helped Dolli better understand the monster she was dealing with. He wanted it all so he could bask in it. So shallow.

The straps to the jar slipped off the wolfkin's shoulders, and Doll's prison dropped to the ground with a thud. The wolfkin kneeled and dropped his head, revealing the monster Kelzoul on a throne of bones and leather.

He was coral-skinned like the other beefslabs Dolli had seen, but he was unquestionably the largest humanoid monster she'd ever laid eyes on. Silvery hair cascaded down his shoulders in beaded braids, and a bone necklace draped his chest. His jaw was wide and square below a thick nose and pale eyes set just a bit farther apart than looked normal.

Kelzoul stood, grinned, and motioned for the wolfkin to rise. The Overlord stepped down the stairs from his throne and approached, towering over the others by at least four feet. He patted the wolfkin with a heavy hand decorated in rings of every metal, inset with a multitude of stones. There was a sword at his hip that appeared to be something a Dusk Knight would wield, and his leggings were worn black leather studded with spikes. His chest was bare—save for the necklace and a single bright pink pauldron. For all the loot he had, he certainly could use some style tips.

The wolfkin stepped aside and gestured to Dolli with a bow, then backed away. Kelzoul picked up the jar with his oversized hand and pulled it up to his face. He tapped the glass a few times.

"Wispelle-proof." Kelzoul's voice was muffled by the glass, but Dolli heard him clear enough. "No slipping out the cracks for you."

Dolli's mind raced as images of her possible futures ran through her head. The Dungeon Core for Monster Haven was safely stored many feet under her hut back in town, but what if Kelzoul could still extract her *yekipyip*—her respawn essence, her anima? This could be the end.

"You come to surrender?" the Overlord asked confidently.

"To make an alliance, actually," she replied. Her voice was loud in the tiny space.

Kelzoul frowned, then looked at the wolfkin. He said something in another language that didn't sound pleased and pointed at the scout that had brought her in. The wolfkin dropped his head, then backed out of the tent while bowing.

Kelzoul walked to the fire and held Dolli's jar over the flames. Uncomfortable heat bloomed around the edges, and Dolli pulled away from the glass. The flames licked up the side of the jar and passed harmlessly over Kelzoul's hands. The air around Dolli felt thick, and the pressure on her body increased.

"You come for what?" Kelzoul asked, then shook the jar. Dolli bounced from side to side, the hot sting of the glass singeing her misty Spark body. It was getting harder to breathe.

"I'm offering you a deal. I can summon heroes," Dolli said with a wheeze.

Kelzoul removed her from the flames and set the jar on a nearby bench. "What use do I have for heroes?"

"Experience, armor, and weapons. We can offer you ten percent of our kills for a mutual understanding that we won't kill each other."

Kelzoul laughed, and the three other coral-skins did too. He gestured about the room and Dolli looked more closely at all the sparkling trophies mounted on the walls. There was a sword glowing blue that sent frost reaching up the wall all around it, a gold helm with tall horns that looked like it had belonged to someone with glorious purpose, an axe with glowing runes on the handle, rings that smoked, on and on.

"I do not need more of their dressings. I do not need the experience. We found a better way."

Orange light drifted through the top of the tent and circled Kelzoul. His eyes went distant for a moment. "Let me show you," he said, grinning.

The orange light circled him faster and faster, like a star caught in the gravity of a black hole. It whipped and flailed as if it were trying to escape him. Kelzoul flexed and bared his teeth. The light touched his skin and wrapped around him, infusing into him and making the exposed parts of his chest a little darker orange.

There wasn't a speck of white on Kelzoul's body, giving Dolli another piece of the puzzle. *He'll eat my yekipyip*, Bakreh's voice returned to her. It wasn't just Kelzoul, but his generals and guards too. The coral skin was from anima consumption.

"You understand my power now?" Kelzoul asked. He looked stronger, bigger, or perhaps it was Dolli's fear making him larger than he was.

"You have what we need. Surrender to us and your strongest get to live."

"But we've only just begun negotiations," Dolli said with a smile. "What about fifteen percent, and a floor in my dungeon?"

Kelzoul grinned, then said something in his language to the others. They chuckled and unsheathed their weapons. This was not at all going the way Dolli had hoped.

"Twenty and two floors. You'll have access to our expert crafters, as well. Alchemy, blacksmiths, architects, enchanted tailors, engineers. We could build you incredible weapons," Dolli said with a flourish of her hands to sell the point.

Kelzoul rubbed his chin in mock thoughtfulness. "What if you keep your twenty percent and I take your core and your crafters? We are short on alchemists… This is the deal I like."

"Well, fortunately for you, I am the Overlord and the Alchemist. I'd provide you with high-quality potions for your escapades."

"That is too bad for you. Your core is the only thing I crave." He licked his lips as one would when thinking of their favorite food.

He didn't care whether she could summon heroes, didn't want her beneficial potions or space in her dungeon. He didn't care about anything she had to offer, except the two things she didn't want to give up: her people and her life.

"We can do it easy, or fun. Which way do you want?" Kelzoul asked with a malicious leer.

"I'd really prefer a third option," Dolli said, then snapped open her menu. She panned to Hero Quests and cursed when she saw the summon button on Keegan was not selectable. Of all the times for him to be unsummonable!

"Oh?" Kelzoul asked with unwavering confidence. Dolli could tell by the way he had patience for the end that he was used to getting his way. He *knew* a little Wispelle like Dolli wasn't going to outmaneuver him. Well, Dolli was happy to surprise.

"How about you leave the valley, and we don't go to war?"

Dolli asked, stalling for more time. The smoke rising from the tent gave her a fraction of a plan, but she needed more.

Kelzoul leaned down. "I promise you can *never* escape my wrath. I am a God-to-be, promised by my ancestors. I am the chosen one, and nothing will stand in my path to immortality."

Dolli shook her head with a scowl. "We're monsters, we're already immortal. What more do you want?"

Kelzoul laughed and picked up Dolli's jar. He moved toward the fire again. "Surrender."

Dolli looked up through Kelzoul's fingers to the hole above. It was pushing a good amount of air, maybe enough to lift her if she used Vapor Conversion to change her shape. The heat in the jar was already uncomfortable, and Dolli knew the way out was going to be even more uncomfortable, but she would survive to take back all the information she'd gathered.

Not just information. Dolli needed one more thing before she could leave.

"Surrender!" Kelzoul shook the jar, jostling her and the dirt around.

"Not to a pathetic excuse of an overlord like you," Dolli said defiantly.

Kelzoul gritted his teeth in a furious leer. "Then it's the fun way."

His grip tightened until the glass cracked, spilling heat and smoke into Dolli's prison. She could escape now, but it wasn't time, not yet. He needed to be blinded by anger, sloppy. He'd killed hundreds, maybe thousands of monsters, and he was confident Dolli would be no different.

She cast Fold Reality at the top of the tent opening and started the twenty-second countdown in her mind. If she didn't cast the second portal by then, the first portal would fizzle, leaving her stranded.

"Suck my balls." Dolli gave him a wink with the rude phrase she'd heard heroes use. Apparently, that was the final straw. Kelzoul twisted the bottom of the contraption open, then reached in for Dolli. She used Burst of Speed to slip past him, then cast Vapor Conversion, transforming into a miniature wyvern. She flowed up his arm to his shoulder, where a silvery braid lay. She chomped down on the dangling hair and ripped a good chunk free.

Kelzoul roared with anger and turned to swipe at Dolli. She dropped over his shoulder and cast the second portal on the ground beside him. She dove headfirst with confidence into the portal, then teleported to the second and rocketed up into the searing jet stream of bonfire fumes.

The hot air pushed her out through the top of the tent, and Kelzoul bellowed commands in his native tongue. The sound of the glass jar shattering followed Dolli into the cold night air, and shards flew past her head. She held tight to the lock of hair while the current of burning heat pushed her higher.

Kelzoul's voice projected throughout the camp. "All flighted units, deploy!"

Dolli was a good forty feet above the tent, but her ascent was slowing. She had to do something, and fast. The Spark bar in the corner of her vision filled a fraction—heck yes for Mortmortis! It was just enough for one more spell.

She angled herself upwards and cast Burst of Speed, then flapped her awkward wyvern wings like mad. She left the jet stream of hot air and moved over the camp. Creatures took flight all around her, none of them much bigger than Dolli, but all of them with full Spark. She was completely out of options—

Or was she?

Dolli summoned one of the Spark potions from her inventory and gripped it in her little clawed hand at the tip of her wing. If she survived this, she'd remember to maintain a few of her more humanoid features like hands. She switched the lock of hair to her other claw, sacrificing a few flaps and dropping a foot.

She downed the potion and her Spark pool refilled to 65%. That would be enough, but would her spells work the way she hoped while in flight? There was only one way to find out.

Two bat-like creatures with horrifyingly long claws came head-on, their leathery wings beating like war drums. Dolli cast Gravity Well in their path with a prayer to the gods. The monsters crossed into her area of effect and instantly slowed, then dropped out of the sky.

An arrow whizzed past her head and Dolli turned to see a short archer in green atop a big flying reindeer with a glowing red nose. The reindeer pranced on the very air, its feet blasting out clouds of white mist where it "stepped." Snow rained down on the camp, giving Dolli some much-needed cover.

"Hurry!" the archer urged, then fired another arrow wide past Dolli's head, spearing an incoming bat.

Dolli stored the lock of hair and the empty bottle in her inventory, then leaned down into the wind and pulled her wings taut. She caught the draft, which pulled her along and lifted her up as cold air caressed her burned wings.

She was almost at the edge of camp when three winged creatures whose round bodies were smooth like polished stone came out of the trees, coasting on the same wind Dolli had caught. She cast Starfire directly overhead, but didn't turn to watch the meteors rain down on her pursuers.

The round blobs of creatures made sounds like angry ribbits, and fireballs belched from their massive mouths. Dolli dipped out of the way and lost her balance, rolling over and over. She'd lost a good twenty feet of elevation before she caught herself, and couldn't gain it again without flying into the trees ahead.

The ribbits that preceded fireballs came again, and Dolli banked, hoping to get out of their path. One clipped her wing and she roared in pain, spiraling out of the sky. A gush of cold air blew pine needles out of the trees and pushed Dolli back up into the air, face-to-face with a real wyvern with its jaws open wide. For a split instant, Dolli felt the panic of imminent death, but then she noticed the blue-green speckles across the wyvern's snout.

"Nubiri!" Dolli cried.

The wyvern dipped her head, catching Dolli, then flapped

hard to regain altitude. Dolli turned and dug her little claws into Nubiri's neck to keep from tumbling down her back and off into the forest. The wyvern's massive maw snapped shut on flesh and bones, eliciting terrified screams from the monsters below.

The giant wyvern pumped her wings and they rose, getting closer and closer to the cloud cover above and well out of the smaller creatures' range. When they breached the tops of the misty white and emerged into the sparkling navy twilight sky, Dolli sighed.

There were a hundred different thoughts running through her mind, but none so important as one. She pulled herself against Nubiri's neck and whispered, "Thank you."

CHAPTER SIX

POISON FOR POTIONS

"How many troops?" Greg asked with a groan. He'd been cradling his face in his oversized hands for the last five minutes as Dolli dished all the details of her capture.

"At least a few thousand. There could've been more to the camp I didn't see," Dolli said, pouring hot water into the third pot of tea. She couldn't enjoy it herself, but it seemed to help keep the others calm.

Nubiri snorted from the open window. "I circled several times; the camp was a mile long with creatures packed into small dens. I would guess four to six thousand."

"Six thousand." Julie whispered the words with disbelief.

Dolli took a seat at the round table they'd set up for these meetings and set the pot of tea in the middle. "Our dungeon just leveled to six, we have two hundred monsters and a maze of epic proportions below our feet. We can overcome them, or at least make the prize so painful they give up."

Rufus blew the air out of his lungs in a big sigh. "We lost about twenty people while you were gone. Defectors. Segrit and Walden among them."

Dolli maintained her cool though the news was a blow. Segrit and Walden were original villagers of Little Crossroads. They were also the dungeon jewelers, having crafted and repaired many interesting pieces for the dungeonfolk.

Greg clenched his fists on the table. "Dirty traitors. This is their home!"

"They may have fled into the forest, but even if they did go to Kelzoul's army, that was their choice. We can't keep them locked in here, but we absolutely cannot let that stop us from doing what's necessary to protect our home."

"What do you mean?" Julie asked with a scowl.

Dolli placed her hand on Julie's. "Kelzoul will send them here to fight…"

"We'll have to kill them," Nubiri finished Dolli's sentence for her.

Julie's eyes went wide and her jaw dropped. "Segrit, Walden, the others… We'll have to kill them?"

"As many times as necessary to protect ourselves," Dolli said with a nod. "But I hope we can prevent war altogether. I have an idea that could easily end this all."

"I won't let you sacrifice yourself!" Rufus said, slamming his fists on the table and rattling the teacups.

Dolli smiled. "I'm glad you feel that way because that's not my plan—not yet at least. We have valuable insight on their camp. Even if they packed up and got on the move tonight, which I doubt, they would have to stop again before getting close enough to Monster Haven to launch an assault. We have an opportunity for sabotage." Dolli smirked, remembering her prize. "I might be able to kill *just* Kelzoul. I got a bit of his hair." She pulled the silvery braid from her inventory and laid it on the table.

"Ew. Why?" Greg asked, his nose wrinkled in disgust.

Dolli's brow arched. "I didn't know you were squeamish, Greg. Our battles could've been over a lot faster had I known that when we were still human."

Greg rolled his eyes. "I'm not. It's just weird. Like a crazy ex-fling casting spells weird—"

"Exactly," Rufus said with a clap. "That's exactly what she plans on doing with it. Dolli, you're a genius."

Greg scowled. "I don't get it. We're going to make him fall in love with us?"

Dolli barked a laugh. "I hadn't thought of that."

"They have to eat," Rufus said with emphasis. "If we could design a poison targeted just at him with that bit of hair, we could poison their water supply or the food, and no one would die but Kelzoul."

"Why not poison everyone?" Nubiri asked.

Julie tutted, serious offense taken. "We would be killing *our friends*. They defected to that camp, remember?"

"Possibly," Dolli said with a shrug. It was very likely. "Moreover, I've known men like him before. Without a doubt, Kelzoul watches his food supply carefully, and someone always eats before him. But in any case, I don't intend to poison the food. We would get a limited window for it to work as food, or it could mess up the targeting if the camp chef used certain herbs," Dolli said grimly. She was a good alchemist, but she couldn't plan for everything. "The point is, there are too many ways for it to go wrong. Disguised as a healing potion though, it could sit for weeks without giving away its nature."

Greg smiled. "Now I'm getting it."

"But he'll just respawn if you poison him, right?" Julie asked.

"I don't intend to kill Kelzoul once. I'm going to destroy his anima, the respawn essence. It'll set all of the dungeon monsters free at once. I'm certain once Kelzoul is truly gone, there'll be a mutiny on the lieutenants' hands, one I'm fully ready to support if they promise to join us," Dolli said, revealing her full, long-term strategy.

She knew the Lifestream-destroying potion she would use to do it, but lacked critical ingredients… and the exact recipe from a book at an abbey deep in hero territory. But hero territory wasn't inaccessible to her.

"I'm going to figure out this potion, and we're all going to bolster our defenses—then get to level ten."

Her council sat in shocked silence.

Finally, Rufus spoke. "It took us weeks to get to level six. How are we supposed to get four more levels in half that?"

Dolli took a long inhale, preparing for their responses. "No more leisure time. We'll put everyone on a new rotating schedule. Combat for five hours, tasks for ten hours, five more hours of combat, then four hours of rest. The extra hour of rest will boost us with an additional 25% XP generation. Since a portion of the earned XP returns to me and the dungeon, we'll level up faster."

No one protested, and a few of them nodded in agreement. Dolli went on. "We have limited time, but I know we can do this. We've survived far worse."

"But what we had to do to survive…" Greg trailed off darkly, his teeth clenched.

Dolli guessed he was talking about the plague and winced. If so, he wasn't going to like the rest of her plan. "I need ingredients, and I'll need an alchemy book from the kingdoms. The heroes are the only way to get that."

Greg growled. "Well, make sure you're the only one mixing the ingredients this time, yeah?"

Everyone was shocked into silence, looking to Dolli for her reply.

She smiled. "Not a mistake I intend to duplicate. Now, there's a lot to do and not a lot of time to do it. Let's get to work."

ALL HANDS ON DECK

Dolli was thankful for all the combat training they'd done the weeks prior. She was especially thankful she'd made it mandatory for all dungeonfolk, no matter their rank, level, or excuses.

"Heroes incoming!" Dolli shouted as she hit the "Mass Summon" button on the recently created quest. The quests were gaining willing heroes more quickly now, and word seemed to be spreading that something was afoot with Monster Haven.

The first hero she'd summoned for a *real* quest had instantly jumped into combat, but with the use of a new trap device Greg made especially for that, she was able to calm him down enough to explain the need. She'd showed him the gold, and even gave him half up front to do the quest. Lo and behold, two hours later the hero had returned with the specified ingredient.

It wasn't what Dolli had needed to get the ultimate winning potion together, but it would allow her to start analyzing Kelzoul's essence. She could discover a lot about him with that lock of hair, and hopefully save her home.

"Three, two, one!" Dolli selected the summon button, and blinding white light filled the catacombs of the dungeon. Twenty heroes materialized, some mid-dance move, others drinking from mugs, and some bloodied from combat.

"It's a battle!" one hero yelled.

"Aw, I wanted an alchemy quest!" another whined.

The Belgruses charged in, rending armor loose and destroying the heroes' stamina. Then the Bronzite stepped up, protecting the Wispelle, Wendigos, and Oakenheart while they laid down various spells.

"Come on! We can do this!" a tall horned hero in the middle of her pack yelled.

These hero fights weren't like the attack made by Keegan's guild. Sure, some of the heroes who accepted Dolli's quests told their friends, and some of the summoned fodder knew one another. But for the most part, these heroes had never fought a single day together. Dolli's troops dominated them in mere minutes.

Dolli moved onto the field, casting Gravity Well on the front-line fighters, then pummeling the crowded group with Solstorm. The bright yellow spell zapped, jumped, and arced its way across the battlefield, healing friends and damaging foes.

At the front, one of her Belgruses had to take over tanking for a critically low Bronzite. Dolli cast Zeal on the quick-thinking dungeonfolk who filled the gap to protect the casters. The bear-like monster grew in size by three feet and flared bright red. That wasn't anything Dolli had done… Must've been his own spell.

Dolli smiled to herself as the heroes screamed and battled with all their hearts to the end. When the fighting was done, Dolli took stock of who remained. She'd lost one Wendigo, but nothing to stop the party from going on. They still had two more hours in their shift, but the dungeon had leveled up and Dolli wanted to take a moment to look over the options.

"Take ten. Replenish your Spark and Health," Dolli said, pointing to the kegs mounted on the wall behind her. "We'll bring in ten this time so we can find our balance. We need to be quick and efficient, and we cannot afford to lose a single one of us."

"For Haven!" Julie said with a victorious cry.

Dolli grinned and raised her misty little fist. "For Haven!"

"For Haven!" the crowd cheered together.

There was an energy in the room that Dolli had never felt before in Little Crossroads. It was as if they were truly connected, bound to one another by the singular goal, the one hope that they would live.

Dolli opened her menu and saw the Hero Quest tab blinking. That would have to wait, as she had dungeon leveling to handle first. When she moved to the Overlord menu, a pop-up appeared.

[Congratulations – Your dungeon has reached Level 7]

Unused Monster Slots: [38/200]
Undistributed Roles: [0/6]
Open Lifestream Slots: [0/6]
Unclaimed Overlord Ability Points: [1]
[3] levels remain until next dungeon ability: Modulate; Resolve.

=====

Dolli saw there was a new item in the Dungeon Abilities menu called [Auto-Complete], which would allow the officers to use Lifestream energy to complete their creations faster or level up their skills. While the Lifewell upgrade blinked at her annoyingly, Dolli felt certain that the new [Auto-Complete] ability would help prepare them for war *now*. She could hope for another dungeon level before the fight for their lives began.

Dolli messaged the officers about the upgrades, which they jumped on eagerly.

That last round of fights had also leveled Dolli up to fifteen. She wasn't entirely miffed that the level up didn't come with any new abilities, since there were several she already had that she wanted to upgrade, like Zeal. She'd used the ability many times but had never had the opportunity to prioritize upgrading it.

[Wispelle Ability: ZEAL]

Spell type: Active
Cost: 75 Spark
Cast time: Instant
Cooldown: 5 minutes
Duration: 1 minute 30 seconds
Range: 20 feet
Target: Self or Friendly / Single Target
Spark Alignment: Divine
Description: Empower your target with the essence of Spark to do great things.
Effects:

- Increase target's Agility, Constitution, Stamina, and Strength by 175%.
- Increase target's Mental Prowess and Magic Affinity by 225%.
- Increase target's Armor Rating by 150%.
- Instantly heal the target by 35% of their total health.

Debuff Disclaimer: When Zeal's duration ends, the target is debuffed with the inverse of all the beneficial stat improvement effects for 10 seconds.

=====

The upgrades going to level two were significant, and she cursed herself for not getting it sooner. Next, she spent her stat points evenly—one each for Constitution, Agility, Mental Prowess, Magical Affinity, and Stamina—then looked over the sheet.

[Dollitrice Grandmeir – Monster Character Sheet]

Name	Level	Alignment
Dollitrice Grandmeir	**15**	**Celestial**
Creature Type	Experience Points	Affiliation
Celestelle	**192**	**Monster Haven**
Health	Health Regen per sec	Carry Capacity LBS
549	**11.15**	**19**
Spark	Spark Regen per sec	Movement Speed Bonus
1423	**42.52**	**14%**
Agility	Constitution	Magical Affinity
12	**21**	**67**
Mental Prowess	Stamina	Strength
68	**18**	**5**
Melee Damage per sec	Ranged Damage per sec	Spell Damage
10.6	**25.5**	**144.5**
Crit Chance	Dodge Chance	Spell Crit Chance
6.75%	**11.14%**	**37.70%**
Armor Rating	Armor Piercing	Celestial Res.
13.00%	**8.50%**	**36.75%**
Divine Res.	Nature Res.	Nether Res.
43.75%	**29.75%**	**35.00%**

======

Finally, Dolli panned over to the blinking Hero Quest menu. One of the fetch quests had been completed and the hero was awaiting turn-in. She selected the Summon button and the room glowed with white.

"Another one!" a dungeonfolk screamed and ran in to attack.

"Wait! This one is for a quest." Dolli blocked the hero from the incoming horde of rabid dungeonfolk. They slowed to a stop, snarling and brandishing weapons.

Dolli turned with a businesslike smile. "I assume you collected everything I asked for?"

"Uh-huh," the hero said, her knees trembling as she clutched her shabby brown robes and gnarled staff.

She was lower level, which was all the more reason why Dolli wanted to help instead of hurt her. Noobs—as the heroes called lower-level heroes—sucked hard at "the game" and weren't allowed to go on big raids. By letting this noob participate in something fun and interesting, Dolli was generating camaraderie with the hero community.

The young mage pulled a weathered, rolled-up parchment and a silken drawstring sack from her inventory and passed them over to Dolli. She inspected the items to confirm they were what she'd conscripted the mage to retrieve.

[Gathmendu's Scroll of Arcane Alchemy]

This is a ripped page from Gathmendu's Tome of Arcane Alchemy. Use to Bind into your own potion recipe book and unlock the recipes.

Those aren't wine stains on the page…

=====

Dolli felt bad for Gathmendu that the hero had torn the page straight out of his book, but whether the mage knew it or not, she'd made the right choice. Most potions had counter-potions inscribed with them, and Dolli most certainly didn't want the antidote to her plan left for someone to find.

She moved on to the brown satchel and inspected the contents.

[Sack of Dolli's Requested Ingredients]

- 1 x vial Grepfel's Gold [Excellent]
- 1 x vial purified moon water from the Lake of Animas [Excellent]
- 1 x Ambrosstone [Good]
- 5 oz Oxine ore powder [Good]
- 2 oz Hempsye leaves [Excellent]

Contents liable to explode. Handle with care. Do not ingest.

======

Dolli beamed. "You've done well, my dear. Let us go get the rest of your reward, as promised." She turned to address the dungeonfolk. "Back in five."

Julie looked worried, her green brow of smoky mist furrowed. She raised a hand to protest, Dolli assumed to say something to the effect of, "It's dangerous to go with the hero alone," but then she lowered her hand with a smile.

Everyone saw or had heard of Dolli's face-off with Keegan. They all knew she was craftier than a cat and as dangerous as a viper when it came to combat. Not only that, but the noob posed absolutely no threat to Dolli.

"My apologies, dear, but may I blindfold you? Don't want you memorizing our layout and telling anyone." Dolli whipped a bit of cloth from her inventory and held it up to the girl.

"Oh, I would never tell." She shook her head earnestly, but then nodded. "I suppose you can never be too careful. Please don't murder me as soon as I put this on."

"If I'd wanted you dead, I wouldn't be wandering off alone with you toward the exit." She passed the mage the blindfold and she tied it in place.

Dolli grabbed her hand and the girl flinched. "Sorry, just a little cold."

They walked in silence for a little way, then the mage couldn't contain herself. "So, I hear you used to, like, be an NPC town, is that right?"

"Yes, we were citizens of Hafheim and became monsters," Dolli said.

"And now you, like, still work with heroes sometimes? How? Is your code broken?" she asked.

"What's your name, dear?"

"It's right over my head," the mage said, pointing to the floating text that read, "Tina_Flamestorm."

Dolli had noticed over the course of farming heroes that sometimes they called one another by different names, less strange things. Pwner420 was actually called Tom, and Lizlacks-Paddiwhacks was called Lizbeth.

"No, dear, your *other* name." Dolli emphasized the word with an audible wink, hoping she'd understand.

"Oh, like, my IRL name? I mean, we're not supposed to tell people online our real names. But I guess since you're just an Overlord and not really a person, it's okay. I'm Katrina."

Dolli didn't particularly like being called "not a person," but supposed this poor noob didn't know any better. "What a lovely name. Mine is Dollitrice Grandmeir, but you can call me Dolli."

"Dolli, I like that a lot. Sounds cute, just like you," Katrina said with a grin.

Dolli chuckled. "I assure you I only look cute. I'm fierce on the battlefield and with a beaker."

"I'm sure you are… You're trying to save your people, right? I mean I've heard rumors, that's why I gambled and accepted the quest."

Fear tickled Dolli's neck. Had she gotten sloppy? She tried to sound amused instead of worried as she asked, "What gave you enough evidence to gamble with painful, gruesome death?"

"*Weeeell*. Okay, so I've been reading the forums a bit because this thing is really starting to take off on *Rebit*, and some people are self-reporting by taking a screencap of their quest, then results: battle or quest. I started putting it together and…"

Dolli stopped. "And what?"

"I know what you're trying to get to."

"Oh, you do?" Dolli asked, amused.

"You want to destroy an essence. A powerful essence. And I have to warn you, it's not really what you think it is!" Katrina said in a hush.

Dolli nodded, then remembered the mage was blindfolded. "Yes, that is my aim, but I assure you, it is safe in my skilled hands."

"Then you know the risk, and why heroes take a chance on it?

It can have some unpredictable effects based on character align-ments and races, even just minor differences cause huge discrepancies!"

Dolli nodded again. "Yes, dear. I know I look youthful but I've had a long life, and have encountered this brew before. I'm confident we have this under control."

They continued on in silence for another fraction of a moment before the talkative energy burst from Katrina again.

"Who are you trying to perma-kill? Keegan?" she asked with a thrill of excitement.

Dolli didn't show her cards. "Why would I want to do that?"

"Because he stole your wyvern's eggs and is hiding them up in his guild tower."

"In his guild tower?" Dolli stopped abruptly, squeezing the girl's hand.

Katrina turned to Dolli and lifted her blindfold. "Yeah, and he shows screencaps off to everyone on his VR-Tube saying how he'll be the first player to have dual wyvern guardians for his guild. I mean Kaxlorick had three *dragons* guarding his guild tower, but I suppose two wyverns is cool."

Dolli's throat was like ash, but her heart felt a glimmer of hope. The children weren't lost to the auction like Keegan had said. She could still get them back.

"You are a fount of wonderful information," Dolli said, returning a smile to her features.

Katrina dropped down to one knee so she was slightly below Dolli's line of sight. "I know as a Witch of the Wilds that must be really painful for you. I'm sorry."

Dolli tried not to let her eyes narrow, or the smile fade from her lips. "How did you know that?"

Katrina shrugged. "Well, I kinda know a lot about *Hafheim Online*. I know, I'm low level. This is just an alt."

Dolli frowned at the word, but urged her to continue with a knowing, "Uh-huh."

"I've been playing since release, ten years, so I'm pretty

knowledgeable. Most of the players have moved to other servers for the Land Beyond the Seas expansion. I dunno if you noticed, not a lotta players around here recently."

"We had indeed taken notice. Part of the reason we're now a dungeon," Dolli said with a nod.

"Wow, that's so cool. We've been coming up with theories of how this happened. I heard the devs are just kinda letting it ride, being coy about who's responsible for this because it wasn't announced or anything! Villages converting into higher difficulty dungeons, it's like new game plus!"

Dolli was putting together the pieces of the Hero Magic event over the past few weeks since they'd transformed. The different names they called one another, calling themselves "players" and Hafheim "the game." Dolli had known Shamans that talked of other realms, places one could see between the air and the sky, connect to different worlds…

Could the Heroes have discovered a way to tap into that magic and open the portals at will?

Katrina took a deep breath, no longer able to contain her rambling spew of knowledge in the silence created by Dolli's thinking. "*Aaaanyway*, most of us think it's some broken code, a bug in the system, and what you just told me gives me a good lead to follow. Polar Games is sort of playing it off like it might be an expansion, or new content, since it's really improving the numbers. Honestly, I'm happy to see the spike in players. The Kingdom of Goreck was getting to be a ghost town, but now my auctions are flying."

Dolli turned back toward the exit, urging Katrina on, despite her blindfold being up. There was a deadline on Kelzoul's arrival, and as much as she wanted to uncover more about the Heroes' Magic, she needed to get back to working on the immediate threat.

Katrina followed clumsily as she pulled her blindfold back in place. "So… what is it? Are you bugged out?"

"I don't know."

They reached the trapdoor exit and Dolli went up first. They made their way toward the treasury, and once inside, Dolli let the mage see the wonders they'd collected: a healthy hoard of weapons, armor, enchanted jewelry, and a small mountain of gold and gems.

"Whoa, this is a pretty decent dungeon stash for level six. It must be true about your increased difficulty level," Katrina said with an approving nod.

"Seven, actually. We just leveled up. And yes, we're quite proud of it. It is well guarded," Dolli added with severity, then retrieved Katrina's reward.

It was a long-sleeved gold-and-orange iridescent flame robe. One of the best pieces of gear Dolli had gotten from a fire mage. It was an appropriate reward for the work Katrina had done. Dolli was certain based on the age of the parchment that it was the original document from the alchemist's lab, not just a copy, and that deserved an equal gift in return.

"Here you are," Dolli said as she flourished the garment with a smile.

Katrina's eyes sparkled. "Wow, the Heartfire Hero's Gown! That's gear from the most recent expansion!"

She took the dress from Dolli and her eyes unfocused.

"Well, dear, if you don't mind, I need to return to *farming*."

Katrina's gaze snapped back to Dolli. "What did you say?" she asked, wholly amused.

"Isn't that what it's called when you slaughter noobs and take their stuff?" Dolli asked.

Katrina squealed. "Oh em gee. No, I mean you're using our *phrases*! The devs have *always* kept the NPCs in character for the realm. This is insane. I'm *sooo* glad I've been screencapping this!"

Dolli smiled, an idea sparking. She could get a lot out of this girl if she just gave a little in return. "How about after we've survived the next weeks, I'll invite you for tea. We can talk all about our worlds together."

Katrina's jaw dropped. "You're not shitting me? For real? I can get *exclusive* access to the reveal? I'm gonna get so many new VR-Tube followers!"

Dolli opened her Hero Quest menu and scrawled out a quick, low-level, low-stakes quest. "Collect one Lillyfern. They're common everywhere in Hafheim. Whenever you're ready to be summoned, complete the quest. It'll alert me to summon you—if I'm still alive."

She targeted the quest at just Tina_Flamestorm. Of course, Katrina could share the quest with her guild, but given the use of the words "exclusive" and "followers" Dolli doubted the mage would want to share any of the glory.

"Ho, lee, sheet…" Katrina said, her mouth snapping shut. She stepped to the side. "I wanna screencap this with you next to the pop-up. This is gonna get mad hits. Everyone is gonna be flocking to my guild for a spot!"

"Yes, well, use this power wisely. Surround yourself with those you trust and nothing can stop you. That bit of wisdom is free of charge," Dolli said with a wink.

"You bet I will. Only the coolest, strongest, most down-to-earth dudes."

Dolli cocked her head. "Earth?"

Katrina grinned. "Oh, yeah, that's the name of my planet. Down-to-earth means to be real."

Dolli nodded, finally understanding. They believed that to be of Earth was the only way to be *real*. That's why Dolli herself wasn't considered "really a person." Katrina believed she was in a land of make-believe, playing a game.

"Interesting. It's been nice talking to someone so down to Hafheim, but now I really must get back to my farming," she said, ushering the girl toward the exit. "Would you like a swift departure by death?"

Katrina grimaced, the smile fading from her face for the first time in minutes. "No, I think I'll just Homecall… thanks though!"

The girl raised her hand, and a burst of yellow light rained down around her, sticking to her body and making it glow. With an audible chime and a whoosh of air, Katrina burst into a thousand golden sparks. The cloud of shimmering dust floated toward the wall and passed through it.

Dolli lingered for a beat, trying to take in everything she'd just learned.

No. No time for that, she reminded herself. She'd have to think about it later when she wasn't about to have her respawn essence sucked out by a mad Overlord. With the scroll in hand, Dolli sped back to the battlefield, counting down the minutes till the end of her shift.

There were murder potions to make.

CHAPTER EIGHT

FIZZLE, POP, BOOM

Dolli tweezed another thread of Kelzoul's hair from the sterilized beaker holding the bunch. She'd cleaned the hair and removed the beads to ensure there were no contaminants interfering with her magic. She didn't want to accidentally target the potion at whoever's blood had last splashed over him.

With practiced care, she brought the hair to her workstation and set it on the metal tray. She took a deep breath and looked at her notes, then the waiting ingredients. She mumbled the steps as her finger traced the page. She pinched the end of the dropper gently, squeezing out just two drops of Firefern sap onto the hair. The silvery strand wriggled and curled in on itself. She sprinkled dried Oriono over the sap, then mushed it together into a cakey mess.

With practiced motions, she moved her goggles into place and clamped tongs on the sides of the metal tray. She moved to her heat-controlled oven and slipped the tray into the top slot, the hottest.

She mentally tapped her nonexistent foot as she counted to twenty. When the tray came free, there was a little pile of smoldering ash sitting at the center. Dolli moved quickly, not wanting any of the essence to escape.

A prefilled vial of liquid starlight waited at the finishing station. Dolli set the tray down on heat pads and scooped a bit of ash into the vial. She corked it and shook the vial in a side-to-side motion to swirl the ingredients together.

Thick orange smoke wafted off the surface of the darkening liquid, and Dolli felt a flicker of hope. Perhaps she'd gotten it right this time. The pressure in the vial mounted, and Dolli pressed her corporeal thumb down on the cork harder.

The vial trembled and Dolli held it still, pushing both thumbs down on the cork to hold it in with a prayer.

The vial shot out the bottom of Dolli's grip with a corky *thhhop* and smashed on the stone floor.

"Bloody widows!" Dolli shouted. She got the broom and mop, then set about cleaning her mess while she muttered curses.

There was a knock at the door and Dolli composed herself. "Yes?"

Rufus poked his head inside. "How is it coming?"

Dolli gestured to the bin full of broken vials, then put her hands on her hips with a sigh. "I'm getting closer. I think I need to make a larger batch so I can use thicker glass and clamps for the cork. That should do it."

Rufus nodded. "Can I help?"

"If you're not busy," Dolli replied. Rufus was always busy, for which Dolli was grateful. He handled much of the restoration schedule and many other important responsibilities so Dolli could focus on the potions, quests, and battles.

Rufus grabbed one of the black aprons hanging on the wall and a pair of goggles. They got to work, this time with larger portions and a bigger vial. Dolli was hesitant to use so much of the limited ingredients—Kelzoul's hair in particular—but she was confident in her solution.

"So, there's been some talk," Rufus started.

"Oh? Juicy rumors about my affiliations with heroes?" Dolli

mused. She mashed the ingredients together, and Rufus opened the oven door for her.

"No, other talk. The dungeonfolk are scared, Dolli."

Dolli hummed. "That's to be expected, but we've been having great success in our battle rotations—nearing dungeon level eight already."

Rufus rubbed the back of his neck. "It's more than that. Some are feeling hopeless. They don't know why you don't surrender yourself to save them."

Dolli jerked the hot tray from the oven and set it at her workstation with a clang. "Well, if they'd seen what I'd seen in Kelzoul's camp, they'd know why."

"I know," Rufus said, exasperated. "I'm telling them why we're doing this, it's just…"

"Not enough," Dolli finished for him. She scooped the blackened powder into the thick potion bottle and corked it, then clamped it with the fire tongs. "Hold this firmly," Dolli said as she passed him the ends of the tongs.

Rufus grabbed hold, and Dolli began the gentle swirling motion. The potion bottle trembled just as the vials had, and the orange smoke filled the empty space. Dolli focused on the potion, willing it to settle. The cork pressed out against the tongs but Rufus held tight. With a burst of light, the ingredients settled. The bottle ceased its trembling and the once blackened liquid was now a dark copper after fusing with the smoke.

"Yes," Dolli whispered. "This should give them some hope, but I know it won't be enough, either. Who's been particularly hopeless? I want them to come with me to deliver the potion."

Rufus scowled. "We agreed this needed to be quick and stealthy. I don't think you should make a field trip out of it just to prove a point."

"I do. If they don't know what we're fighting for, they won't fight hard enough. If they know there's another option, they'll give in instead of doing what's hard—I know from experience."

Rufus looked down, his brow furrowed with pain and frustration. "Dolli, this doesn't seem smart."

"I'll take three more, only doubling the party size. Stealth only: Stagarth, Noctaves, and Destratos. We'll be quick and go unseen."

"If you fail—"

"We will all die, I know!"

They were quiet for a moment as the flare of anger dissipated. Dolli set the potion on the table and took a deep breath. "I'm sorry, but if they don't understand, Monster Haven will fare worse than death. Half the dungeonfolk will be enslaved and worked to the bone. The other half will have their anima sucked out to fuel that monster's wrath. No Hafhaven, no Nevheröld, nothing. Just part of Kelzoul forever."

Rufus set the tongs down and put a hand on Dolli's shoulder. "You're trying to do what's best for them, I get it. But is showing them the camp and risking this quest what's best for them?"

She thought of all the options, all the outcomes. If they couldn't believe her and Nubiri, or the fear in poor Bakreh's eyes, how would they know what was at stake? How would they fight as if their animas truly depended on it if they thought there was another way where just one person—Dolli—sacrificed themselves? If it was that simple, Dolli would've done it already.

She didn't want to die, but even more, she didn't want her people to suffer. They had to feel that same drive. They had to understand why she was doing this for them.

"Yes. I believe this is the right thing to do. We won't fail, but if we do, I know we can come up with another plan. Look at all we've been able to do in just a few days," Dolli said, pride swelling as she thought of everything they'd accomplished. They had to be unified. They had to stick together through this.

Rufus nodded. "We've lost another group of dungeonfolk, Vilhelm and Henrietta among them."

Dolli dropped her head, allowing the weight of his words to show through in her exhaustion. She was coming up on her twenty-four-hour mark and needed rest, soon.

She pulled herself together and looked Rufus in the eyes. "They're just the same as the other defectors. They won't stop us from doing what needs to be done to save Monster Haven."

Rufus nodded. "I just thought you'd want to know."

"Thank you." She took a seat on a nearby stool. "I need to rest in the Lifestream. Select two or three higher-level stealthers to come with me, some of those who may not be feeling so good about our plan."

"It'll be done, Overlord." Rufus dipped his head.

Dolli opened her Overlord menu in half her vision, watching Rufus leave in the other. She eyed the "Recall" button next to her name and watched him go. The door slammed, leaving Dolli in silence with a final echoing thought: what if she'd never been Regnant? Where would her people be now?

She shook her head. The thought was useless. Too many possible scenarios could've come from the plague event alone to know where they'd be now. She had to do the best she could with what she had, and save as many lives as possible. Just like with the plague, inaction was the only wrong path. She wouldn't sit around waiting for doom to come to her doorstep.

One way or another, Dolli would put an end to Kelzoul.

CHAPTER NINE

UNDERBRUSH ESCAPADES

Nubiri sliced through the frigid night air, the currents lifting her strained wings. They'd been coasting on the wind for over a mile since the warmonger's camp came into view. They didn't want to alert any of their especially watchful night guards. Kelzoul knew Nubiri was with Monster Haven, so there was bound to be someone watching the sky.

"Lower," Dolli whispered in Nubiri's ear. The wyvern dropped her head and angled down. They accelerated and drew closer to the tree line.

"Get ready," Dolli said just loud enough for the two gripped in Nubiri's claws to hear.

Brene, now a towering Stagarth, gripped Dolli's shoulder. Her look said it all: "Civilians on a military mission? Really, Overlord?" But what Brene didn't understand was that none of them were "civilians," not anymore. They all had to be ready for war, and showing them the horrors of it was the fastest way she knew to prepare them.

The flickering firelights of Kelzoul's camp became obscured by the treetops, and Dolli knew it was nearly time. "Thanks for the ride, Nubiri," Dolli said. She opened the Overlord menu and selected to return Nubiri to the Lifestream. The wyvern was well overdue on her exhaustion debuff, but she was essential to this leg of the plan. Getting them to the camp with speed under cover of darkness was the only way the whole thing worked.

The wyvern disappeared in a burst of green, and gravity took the riders. The Noctave—Toren—unfurled wings so deep blue they looked black. He caught the draft and pulled up against the fall. Leina shifted her skin, transforming it into coarse sand. She threw a platform of golden sand out in front of her, stepping down with dancer-like grace. The platform disappeared and another materialized in front of her.

Dolli locked a hand around Brene's antlers and aimed her first portal for Fold Reality just above the trees. Before they could pick up too much downward momentum, Dolli threw the second portal directly in their path. They slipped between the fold, instantly jumping down thirty feet.

Brene extended her arms, reaching out for the forest around her. Mossy vines shot out from her fingertips, and she snagged the first branch below the canopy. They swung through the trees with a quiet *whoosh* before Brene caught herself on a thick branch. They were high enough that there were likely no traps, and they could travel quietly to avoid patrols—Dolli hoped.

Toren sailed overhead, then folded his wings as he came in to land on the branch in front of them. Leina skipped across her sandy stepping-stones and came to a stop next to him. Dolli looked at Brene, beaming with pride. They weren't civilians anymore. They were stealthy assassins come in the night to protect their home.

Brene gave a conceding shrug, then cast a quick Creeping Moss on Dolli, pinning the Overlord to her shoulder. Dolli could be concealed by Brene's camouflage magic if she was wrapped securely in her control spell, an upgraded modification Brene had specifically selected for this mission.

Dolli was the only person who could navigate Kelzoul's camp. Though he would've been smart to rearrange it, Dolli knew he wouldn't. Kelzoul didn't consider Dolli a real threat, and rearranging the placement of the camp would be a logistical night-mare days before a battle.

When Dolli was secured against Brene's shoulder, they all slipped into the shadows of their stealth abilities. Dolli opened her map and the message system side by side.

The map was lit up like a bonfire to the southeast, indicating a massive enemy force. Dolli scrawled off a quick message to the monsters in her vicinity. *Stay within twenty feet of one another, heading southeast.*

She watched the map as the little dots representing the four assassins moved through the trees. *Good, let's pick up the pace. Brene, take the lead.*

Leina and Toren slowed and dropped back, letting Brene get to the front. They were far more organized from the past few weeks of battle than Dolli could've ever hoped for. Could they have been this powerfully synchronized as a village of citizens?

Sounds of combat training and weapon smithing seeped through the trees, and Dolli knew they were getting close. The red on her map came into view as twenty-five little splotches. One of the splotches was moving slowly, but the others were stationary. Dolli tapped Brene's shoulder twice and she slowed to a stop, then crouched.

Dolli closed her menu and surveyed the opening ahead. They'd chopped back only as many trees as they'd needed to put up their structures. Things were tighter, buildings packed between interspersed groves. Dolli couldn't have hoped for a more perfect setting for their infiltration. She gave Brene another single tap to have her move forward.

No one would ever know they were there, and Kelzoul would drink his potions on the battlefield none the wiser of their taint. Just one would do it, and the warmongering Overlord's mind would be banished to Nevheröld, leaving his body a withering husk to which he couldn't return.

They made it to the edge of the trees where a fork navigated around this clearing of blacksmiths and combat yards. Goblin creatures swung their swords at the stumps left from their housing and fuel needs. One of the taller, coral-skinned creatures paced among them, shouting commands. The goblins swung, chopped, and pretend parried in unison to his orders.

Brene came to a stop, giving Dolli a gentle *tap-ta-tap* that asked, "Where to now?"

Dolli opened the menus and checked the map, then gave her orders. *West around this section then south. We'll check the next groves to make sure we're heading **in** and not just **around**.*

They made their way over the treetops in silent invisibility. They slowed every so often when Leina or Toren fell behind, taking in the horrifying sights. There was no laughter, no revelries like back in Monster Haven. There were no hobbies, friendships, or play. No children.

After a few moments of this exposure, they became even more driven. Fire burned through Dolli's belly at the injustice of the place, and it wasn't all her own. Her people felt it too, making Dolli's convictions even stronger. They would be unified again. They would stand a chance against this monstrosity, Kelzoul.

Not far from Kelzoul's luxurious torture tent, Dolli spied the building she knew was his private store. The flap door to the building was marked with a rough depiction of Kelzoul's face, covered in blood and giving a wicked war cry.

Dolli opened her chat menu. *This is it. Remember, I will shapeshift into one of the coral-skins, then Fold Reality to get back up when the deed is done. If I'm caught, kill me, then kill yourselves if you can't escape. You do not want to be held captive by this man —*

A horrified scream broke through Dolli's message. It was Henrietta, and Dolli could just barely make out the words. "Don't know anything! I would tell you!"

Kelzoul's voice was too quiet for Dolli to hear, but Henrietta replied in a wail seconds later. "The layout changes, and the Wispelle, Julie, she's the architect... I don't know. Ah!"

Dolli breathed slow and steady through her nose. She felt the desire to burst down the door and lay waste to Kelzoul, and their little ragtag crew might even be able to pull it off—

But that wasn't the end game. Killing him would do nothing. He'd respawn in a few hours and Dolli would've wasted her shot to end it for good. The desire burned hotter, and Dolli knew it was that of her people. They wanted to murder Kelzoul for touching their own.

Leina pulled up close to Dolli and Brene, whispering, "We have to do something."

Below them, a coral-skinned patrol looked up with puzzlement, then marched on. Dolli let out a held breath and opened her menu. *We are doing something. We're preventing this from happening to* all *our people.*

"He's butchering her," Toren whispered, his voice a deep growl of hatred.

We can't sacrifice killing him for good to save her.

"Heartless," Leina whispered. "Just like you always were." She leapt from the treetop and raced through the air across the clearing to Kelzoul's tent. The guard at the front gate looked up with a quizzical tilt of her head, squinting.

Dolli's body turned to ice. In a flurry, she opened the Overlord menu. She scrolled to Leina's line, trying to return her to the Lifestream—but she was already in combat.

The first guard nudged the second, then pointed up with a foreign command.

Leina landed on the wooden post with a puff of sand, then put herself against the wall and shifted her skin. She didn't match the wood color, not closely enough to fool Dolli at this range, but it could be enough to stump the guards.

The mission. She had to finish the mission.

"Let me down," Dolli whispered to Brene.

The guards stepped back from the gate and looked up at the wall where Leina had landed.

Dolli used Vapor Conversion and changed her form to mimic the lesser guards, then swapped her powerful gear out for the loincloth the apprentice tailors had made specially for this mission.

"Good luck," Brene whispered, then held a near invisible viny-rope out to Dolli. If she'd had a heart, it would've been hammering out of her chest. Instead, Dolli felt pins and needles all over her too-real skin.

Dolli took the rope and dropped down the back side of the tree trunk into the underbrush. She adjusted the loincloth, necklace, and bracers, then walked onto the main path as if she belonged there.

"I saw something," the first guard said to the second.

"A bird?" the second asked.

The first guard hit him upside the head. "None at night."

"Owl."

"No."

"Hmm, bat then?"

"No, it was bigger than a bat. It was a gold cloud."

The second guard grunted a laugh. "A blessing from the Great Spirit for Kelzoul's victory."

"Or an assassin," the first hissed.

Dolli walked behind the guards as they searched the wall for Leina and pulled back the flap to the storeroom.

The first guard spun around with a start, brandishing her spear. "What business you got here?" she demanded, sticking the pointy end under Dolli's chin.

Dolli tried to match their speech from the limited exposure she'd had. "Fillin' up potions—"

Henrietta screamed, ripping at the air with her terror and interrupting Dolli's thought. Dolli stammered, then pulled several health potions from her inventory and showed them to the guard's scrutinizing eyes.

Dolli went on. "High quality. He'll want them for the battle."

"You sayin' he needs them?" The guard poked the spear tip into Dolli's throat.

"No! No. Overlord is powerful. But maybe he flaunts his

power and gets weak dungeon to surrender." Dolli overacted her subservience, hoping to appease the coral-skin.

"Give me one." The guard pulled one of the health potions from Dolli's open hand. She held the vial up to the firelight and inspected it, as if she knew what she was doing. Dolli had to contain a smirk as the guard nodded approvingly, then grunted for Dolli to enter the storeroom.

"I see something," guard number two said, pointing his spear directly at Leina.

Dolli averted her gaze and returned to her mission. Leina, just like Henrietta, had made her choice, and it was hers to deal with. The potion store couldn't be suspected, and neither could Dolli.

The canvas flap fell shut behind her and Dolli took in the storeroom. Everything was under lock and key. *Everything*. Dolli cursed under her breath, but started working the problem.

If she used Fold Reality to get into one of the chests, she could plant the poison, but then she'd have no way out. She'd also have no idea if the chest she was breaking into was full of potions, food goods, gear, or whatever else. She could go ask for the key or try to lift it off the distracted guard.

"Do it," the guard's muffled voice caught Dolli's attention, and the pained shout of Leina broke through her train of thought.

"Get her! Ah! Above us!"

Now it was all going to Nevheröld.

CHAPTER TEN
HARD CHOICES

"There's another one!" the male guard yelled outside the tent.

Dolli was running out of options. Perhaps if she left them on top of one of the crates, the next person to come in would put them away without a thought? It was all she could hope for.

Dolli rushed to an iron-bound chest and set the five health potions on top with a quick prayer. She looked up, trying to cast her first portal out into the tree line above, but got a negative buzzing in her ears instead.

[No Line of Sight]

You cannot cast that spell without line of sight.

=====

Damn it all!

Dolli snuck to the edge of the tent and peeked through the gap in the canvas. Toren swooped down and ripped the spear out of the male guard's hands, then snapped it in his claws. Leina had the female guard wrapped in sand and was squeezing the life from her eyes. They'd soon have two dead guards right outside the provisions tent—not a good look for their plan.

"Help!" The male guard got out one good cry that surely resonated far enough to draw attention.

Dolli jumped from the tent and pulled the dagger from her belt.

The guard pointed to Leina. "Get the shifter!"

Dolli nodded and moved around behind the guard, then stabbed the dagger through the meat of his leg and ripped down. The guard fell to his knees and Dolli pulled the cold, jagged steel across his throat, silencing him.

"A little late, Overlord," Toren said. He swooped low and dragged his claws across the female guard, who was gasping for air. Blood sprayed through the shifting sands, and she crumpled to her knees.

"We can't have the provisions under suspicion. We must assault Kelzoul himself. Find the key," Dolli said, rolling the male guard over. He didn't have anything on him.

"There, right there!" came a shout from down the path. Three goblins pointed with bony fingers to Dolli and her not-so-stealthy comrades. The coral-skinned creatures pushed the goblins aside and charged forward.

"Not good," Toren said, then took to the sky.

Brene dropped from the tree with a dirt-trembling thud and dashed antlers-first into the new attackers. She speared one of them through the chest and shook her head to toss him to the ground.

"Got it!" Leina called and jingled the keys between her fingers.

Dolli dropped her corporeal form, taking on the misty glow of her Celestelle body. With a single gulp she downed one of the untainted restorative potions she'd saved for herself, refilling her Spark to 75%.

Dolli snatched the keys from Leina's hand with a nasty glare. The only way to play this off now was to pretend it was a rescue mission all along. Kelzoul didn't seem like the brightest candle in the cathedral, but he'd made it this far as a dungeon slayer, so he had to have a decent sense of self-preservation.

Dolli twisted the key in the lock and the gate groaned open. Leina screamed when she saw the torture chamber full of Dolli's dungeonfolk. The flayed corpses of Henrietta, Segrit, and many more twisted Dolli's guts. Leina rushed to Henrietta's side, sobbing apologies and curses.

Where was Kelzoul? Dolli scanned the clearing, trying her best not to take in the horrific sight. He must've retreated to his seat of power, but all this noise would surely draw him out. They had to be swift.

"Dol—trice." A weak voice gave Dolli a start. She turned to see what poor creature had tried to utter her name. An Osorath, dismembered down to a bleeding abdomen and sunken skull, stared back at her from one of Kelzoul's tables. Fury, fear, and devastation erupted in her mind.

Dolli pulled a health potion from her inventory and held it to Vilhelm's bruised lips. "Drink," she commanded.

Sounds of the battle outside the gate grew louder, and Dolli knew Brene and Toren couldn't hold them off much longer—then there was Kelzoul, wherever he was.

The magic of the potion dripped out the bottom of Vilhelm's chest and drained from his arm stumps. Dolli clenched her jaw in frustration.

"He took it," Vilhelm uttered in a ragged breath.

"Your respawn essence?" Dolli asked.

Vilhelm nodded.

Dolli watched helplessly, fury burning through her body. The glow of her twilight colors ran red and her body pulsed like an angry beacon.

"You were a fool," she hissed at the dying Osorath, then placed a hand on his blood-drenched face. "I'm so sorry."

"Don't let 'm do… more."

Dolli nodded. "I won't. Close your eyes now, and dream of Hafhaven."

"Thank... ew." His eyes fluttered shut and a grateful smile graced his lip.

Dolli summoned an icy Spark Lance and pushed it through his heart. Frost climbed up and down Vilhelm's body, and he sighed his last breath.

"What are you doing?" Leina shrilled and covered Vilhelm's body in a protective layer of sand.

"He'd had his essence removed, there was no saving him."

"Did you even try?" Leina yelled through her tears.

"I did the only things I could." She threw the empty health potion to the ground. "We need to leave, or we'll be joining him."

"Overlord!" Brene yelled from the battle at the gate.

Dolli grabbed Leina's hand and pulled her from the gore-filled antechamber. Three coral-skins lay dead on the ground but five more of them had joined the fray. Dolli cast Gravity Well, followed by Zeal on Brene, and finally Solstorm. The chain of yellow power jumped from Dolli to Brene, then bounced around between the enemies.

"Into the trees!" Dolli yelled. She knew with this commotion, reinforcements were surely on the way.

Brene was still fighting, her health low. "I'll stay. You go!"

Leina, Toren, and Dolli all had ways to fly, but Brene relied on stealth. The Stagarth had no way to escape now, other than death. There was no time to come up with another plan. Dolli cast the first portal directly in front of her, and the second on a low, thick branch. She pulled Leina through the portal with her and spared a second for another Spark potion.

Leina dropped to her knees, tears streaming down her shifting sandy cheeks. "I can't do it."

There was no time for breakdowns either.

Dolli barked with her Overlord presence, "Move or die!"

Leina yelped and jumped to her feet, quivering. She threw her sandy shield out and jumped onto it, then another, until she was climbing into the dense vegetation of the forest. Dolli followed behind, using Burst of Speed to keep up.

"We're just going to leave them?" Toren cawed angrily beside Dolli.

"They're dead! Forever dead!" Dolli snapped.

A loud ribbit echoed through the trees and the crackling sound of a fireball rushed toward Dolli. She dove off the sandy platforms and clung to a nearby branch as the fireball blazed past and exploded on the tree trunk next to Leina. She shielded herself from the blast, and the sand turned to glass, dropping to the ground with a loud shatter.

They were going to aggro the entire camp at this rate! Dolli thought of killing Leina and Toren to save them the trouble, but a misty white presence in the branches stayed her hand. A glowing red nose led the way for nine little elves on nine floating reindeer. Snow blanketed the forest floor, covering the troops advancing on Brene.

"Needin' a ride?" the lead elf asked. He extended a hand to Dolli with a winning smile.

Dolli looked down. Brene was fighting on, her health bar critically low. Dolli didn't want to leave without watching her die. She couldn't let Brene be captured and tortured like the others.

"My dungeonfolk!" she said, no time to convey the full message.

The elf looked down, then drew an arrow to his bow as quick as lightning. The tip of the arrow glowed blue, then little ghosts of ribbons and bells danced around it. He loosed, and the shot whistled through the air with a merry jingle. The arrow penetrated deep into Brene's shoulder, down to her heart, and burst in a shower of silver ribbons. Brene dropped to the dirt, then burst into green sparks and floated up in the air as if daring Dolli to race home.

"Ready now?" the elf asked again, hand extended to her.

Dolli took it and he pulled her onto the reindeer.

"I'm Taffy," he said, grabbing the creature's reins.

Another fireball blasted through the trees and Taffy whipped the reindeer into action. The creature took off with blinding speed.

Dolli grabbed a fistful of the elf's vest to keep from flying off, then pulled herself close.

"Dolli. Thank you," she said, her body on pins and needles.

The elf barked a sarcastic laugh. "Alright, Doll, don't be jinxin' us before we're clear!"

Shouts from the camp below followed them into the night, but the heavy snowfall and great speed kept the other flying creatures from catching up. They broke through the trees and into the pink sky.

The horrors of the torture chamber returned to her, but instead of Kelzoul's camp, it was Monster Haven. Her dungeonfolk lay butchered in the streets, shouting for mercy and begging for the end. The children screamed for their parents and friends, helpless to do anything but watch.

Dolli closed her eyes and let the whistling wind blow away those fake horrors. She'd never wanted any of this, but gods be damned and stripped of their magic, she would *not* let Kelzoul take another dungeon, or another life. She would put an end to him for good.

CHAPTER ELEVEN

ELVES ON THE WIND

I t had only been an hour since their daring escape, but already Dolli could see the top of Monster Haven's tower highlighted in early pink sunlight behind the mountains. Whenever the pack slowed, Taffy—the lead elf—began a chant of "Ho, ho, ho!" and the reindeer galloped into action. It was as if the whip of a cruel master were at their backs.

Horror images played in Dolli's mind over and over, so to block them out, she opened her Overlord menu to distract herself.

[Congratulations – Your dungeon has reached Level 8]

Unused Monster Slots: [49/200]
Undistributed Roles: [0/6]
Open Lifestream Slots: [4/6]
Unclaimed Overlord Ability Points: [1]
[2] levels remain until next dungeon ability: Modulate; Resolve.
Ascension Boost: The dungeon will now grow by 25 feet per level.

=====

It troubled her that the unused monster slots number had grown... but that was just a fact of their lives. Some of the new recruits, and even her own people, were too scared to stand and fight. Some had defected, not yet knowing the fate of the others.

Dolli moved on to the Overlord Abilities. There was nothing new, and the Lifewell upgrade was still gnawing at her, so she selected that and moved on quickly. There were two messages in the chat system when she panned to that menu.

Rufus: *Hero influx has slowed overnight. I've moved everyone to building reinforcements but we're running out of materials.*

Greg: *We need to start mining the mountains. I'll send my apprentice out if you can divert a few dungeonfolk to protect him.*

There were no other replies, so Dolli assumed they'd met up in person to figure it out. She took a deep breath of crisp morning air and closed the menus.

They came around the final hill down into the valley where the village of Little Crossroads once sat. Now, Monster Haven's ninety-foot-tall tower stood in its place, bathed in the colors of the rising sun. Even at a distance Dolli could see Haven was awake and busy.

With no need to sleep, they'd transformed much of the upper village into public crafting and hobby areas. Of course, with Kelzoul on the way, those had quickly been re-transformed into training areas, traps, and weapon mounts. The night-watch had their freshly upgraded ballistae trained on Dolli and her group as they galloped into town. The reindeer landed on the main road with a clattering clop that echoed across the reinforced buildings.

Rufus, Greg, and a small army of Osorath met Dolli at X Marks the Spot.

Dolli dismounted and bowed to Taffy. "We're in your debt for such a daring rescue."

Taffy blew a raspberry. "Save the pleasantries, we ain't staying."

The elf's strange accent and cavalier attitude was unlike anything Dolli had experienced. It wasn't just Taffy's accent that was strange, but his clothes, his magic, and his weird reindeer, too. He couldn't have been from anywhere near the five kingdoms, that was for sure.

Dolli collected herself. "I was simply thanking you."

Taffy leaned to the side and rested his elbow on his knee and his face on his hand. "The very next question was gonna be, 'Ey, why dontcha hang 'round and stick it to the old Overlord?' Wasn't it?"

Dolli smiled calmly. "Well why don't you? I have a method to kill him, forever, and if you stay and fight, we'll protect you."

"Didja hear that, fellas? She's gonna protect us from him," Taffy said. He turned to the others, and they chuckled.

"Yeah, heard that one before," a female elf said with a scoff.

Taffy turned back to Dolli, his fake smile faded. "Look, lady, we used you. We've been wanting out of that dungeon for months and your little antics were the perfect distraction."

"You could've left, but you didn't," Dolli retorted.

Taffy waved away the comment. "You're reading into it. I wanted extra firepower, or *bargaining chips*, for the escape."

Dolli hardened to him. "He'll hunt you and every other dungeon in Hafheim until they're all his. If we don't stop him now, there may be no stopping him ever."

"Slasher's faster than any of his best fliers," one elf said, patting her reindeer—Slasher—on the neck. The beast leaned into the touch affectionately, and the elf scratched behind its ear.

"You'll run forever, then?" Rufus asked, coming to Dolli's side. The male skolf was hanging off his shoulder, sniffing at the elves and reindeer with a snarl on its face.

Taffy backed away from the oversized weasel with a scowl. "If we have to."

"You could make a home here," Dolli offered. "We pursue our passions, make families, have festivals… we *live* here."

Taffy shrugged nonchalantly. "Look, that sounds pretty nice and all, but you guys don't stand a chance. We've seen him murder dozens of dungeons, at least half of 'em more powerful than you. We can't be dyin' for some dungeon we hardly know."

Rufus opened his mouth to protest, but Dolli stopped him. "No, he's right." She looked to Taffy. "You didn't have to save us, but you did. Whether it was selfish doesn't matter, we must repay that debt. Let us feed and equip you before you go."

The elves glanced between one another again, then stroked their reindeer's manes. The reindeer stamped their feet and bleated. Still, they looked wary of the offer.

"Not sure it's such a good idea," Taffy replied. Dark circles ringed his eyes like he hadn't slept in a day or two, and the rest of his company didn't look much better.

"You may not get another chance to eat and rest for days," Dolli pressed. "Kelzoul won't be here for another few days."

They exchanged a few more glances, then Taffy dismounted. "We gladly accept if we can be quick. Is there anywhere the reindeer could feed and get shoed?"

Dolli passed the request off to Greg, who nodded. "I'll take the reindeer."

"Rufus, could you pour us some ale?" Dolli asked her friend with a bright smile.

Rufus seemed to get Dolli's intention without missing a beat— or perhaps he thought she was still trying to convert them, she wasn't sure. Either way, Rufus nodded and led on to his inn. "Do you prefer light or dark ales, Mr..."

"Dark, and it's just Taffy," the elf said as he swaggered up beside Rufus. "That's Peppermint, Truffle, Ginger, Caramel, Cookie, Nog, Fudge, and Gumdrop." He pointed to the other elves in turn.

The elves were only a half foot taller than Dolli, and only came up to Rufus' waist, but they walked with the confidence of an Osorath. Hollow bells attached to their shoes clanked together without a jingle as they walked into the inn. They found a long table that could fit everyone, and Rufus went to the bar.

Dolli took the seat next to Taffy. "How long were you with Kelzoul?"

Taffy's face wrinkled in disgust. "Too damn long. We never got ale, either. Been years since we've tasted a good brew."

"Ours is decent. We were recently a village of citizens, and when we transformed into a dungeon, we lost all our skill. Had to start over."

"A village of *NPCs*, huh? How'd this happen to ya?" Taffy asked.

"I was negligent. My village suffered a plague, then a severe reputation hit, then another, and another. I stopped putting in the work and hid from them until almost everyone had left. Then one day I got a notification that said we'd turn into a dungeon. Now here we are."

"And you had to restart from scratch? Yeesh, that sounds rough. Good thing though. Kelzoul doesn't spare villages neither, and they're prime pickings for restocking supplies."

Rufus came back to the table, balancing two platters stacked with beers and bread. He distributed the drinks, then held up his own for a toast. "To new friends, even if you're not staying long."

"Thanks," Taffy said before diving into his drink. He took it in huge gulps, groaning with satisfaction every time he swallowed. In just a few seconds, their cups were emptied.

Rufus blinked in surprise. "I'll get a pitcher."

Dolli couldn't waste any more time. "So, what monsters does Kelzoul usually send first? What are their abilities?"

Taffy held out a hand to stop her as he chewed a huge hunk of bread. "Whoa, whoa, whoa. I thought this was a gesture of thanks?"

Dolli shrugged. "You also used me and killed my guard."

"I did her a favor, which ain't somethin' we hand out all the time."

Dolli sighed in frustration. "Wouldn't it be nice not having to look over your shoulder every morning? Your information could help us defeat him."

"You, defeat him?" Taffy laughed, then glugged down his second pour. He slammed the cup down and belched loudly.

Dolli caught Rufus' eye as everyone else focused on their bread and beer. She mouthed, "Stew," and Rufus gave a discreet nod. While they didn't *need* to eat, Rufus had discovered that food came with interesting bonuses for a limited time—some of them very beneficial.

"Look, you seem like a nice Overlord, and that's great and all, but Kelzoul is gonna be here in three days, maybe four if he takes his time. He's going to wash this place in blood and steal your animas—you can't stop him. He's gonna come looking for information about the *escapees* though, and the less you can tell him about us, the better."

Dolli made a mental note of the timeline but didn't pin her survival on it. Kelzoul could move faster if he sent a smaller detachment of forces.

"What if that information can stop him? Wouldn't that be worth the risk?"

Taffy shot her a look of sympathy. "No, because your chances are *that bad*. I'm not tryin' to be an asshole, just sayin' it like it is. He's level forty-five and all his generals are in the high thirties. He's got unbelievable dungeon abilities—some real shit-your-pants type stuff."

Rufus came with the stew and Dolli let Taffy get a few bites. He held the bowl so close to his mouth Dolli thought he might start drinking it from the edge to get it down faster.

When their feasting slowed, Dolli spoke again. "I've been doing some math and I think you're right: we're all going to die. What can I do to save some of them?"

"Tell 'em to run, like us," Taffy said with a shrug. "Few day's head start, some of 'em will get away, at least for a while. Eh, and you could always try sacrificing yourself."

"One of the monsters, Bakreh, told me I could do that. Is that how you survived?"

Taffy seesawed his head. "Sure. Our Overlord sacrificed

himself. That got a few of us in, but everyone else… our whole dungeon was wiped out like that"—he snapped his fingers. "We were the most difficult dungeon in the Frost Bane expansion, and he steamrolled us! I mean… *them.*"

"What happened?" Dolli asked in a gentle tone.

Taffy's gaze was a hundred miles away. "He made us fight at the front to demoralize the others. They didn't want to hurt us. Made it easier for Kelzoul to sneak 'round back and climb the North Pole tower, unseat the Missus… She didn't go down without a fight though, I'll tell you what!"

One of the other elves—Cookie—raised her glass and said, "She nearly plucked the dungeon core right outta his chest!"

They all laughed for a moment, a long-forgotten memory come to bring them fleeting joy.

Taffy's brow furrowed. "If only we'd defeated him then, when we stood a chance. Was the big guy really that bad? Kelzoul bad, I mean?"

The mood at the table got somber.

"We did what we had to," Cookie said, putting a hand on Taffy's forearm.

Dolli felt she was missing some serious context, but didn't press the matter.

Taffy shook his head and took another long pull of ale.

Dolli poured him a bit more. "His dungeon core is inside his body? His chest?"

Taffy bobbed his head and drank back what she gave him.

"Do you think he'll use that demoralizing tactic on us? We've had a few defectors, though I saw some of them have already been killed."

Taffy nodded, his gaze still unfixed and wandering. "Without a doubt. It's his number one tactic."

He gulped back the last of the ale then belched loudly. "He'll take the animas of the strongest defectors—doesn't want an internal uprising before the battle gets underway. He tortures them for information first, in front of the weaker ones to strike fear in 'em."

The way he spoke, Dolli knew Taffy had lived it before.

"Then he'll put those fear-stricken weak ones up front in the battle. Unless you're one'a his, he'll eat you when you die. Dyin' in Kelzoul's army is a one-way trip to juicin' him up."

Dolli remembered the orange essence that floated around him, the way it had fought as if it were trying to escape.

"Every battle could be your last. Made us all desperate, mad even."

"That sounds horrible," Dolli said, putting a misty hand on his forearm like she'd seen Cookie do earlier.

"Yeah well, we're out now, and I've spilled the beans that might split my skull." Taffy sniffled and shook Dolli's hand from his arm so he could take another drink, but his cup was empty. He looked at the bottom of the mug, then stood. "We best be on our way."

His posse followed suit, finishing up whatever they had. Some were shoving hunks of bread into their pockets and others downed the last bits of ale from the tankards.

Dolli walked him out to the main street and asked for their reindeer from a passing goblin. He nodded and ran off toward the stables.

"Wow, you've really got some diversity in here," Taffy noted with a hint of suspicion.

"We don't call it Monster *Haven* for nothing. Everyone is welcome here."

The reindeer came trotting down the street, apparently revitalized by their short break.

"We wish you a safe journey," Dolli said with a smile that belied her fear.

Taffy mounted his reindeer, then trotted to her side. He leaned down and looked at her gravely. "When he thinks he's won, he'll come struttin' in here to kill you himself. I hope you've got a trick up your sleeve for when the time comes."

"Me too." Dolli didn't know how she was going to get Kelzoul low enough health to drink a potion, but at least she had that advantage. They knew what they had to do, and they'd figure it out.

Taffy turned his mount and galloped down the main street. White mist gathered at the reindeer's feet, and they took off into the sky, walking on air. Dolli didn't have time to watch them go. There were battle preparations to be made, two more dungeon levels to achieve, and plans to be forged.

CHAPTER TWELVE

SUICIDE, SELF-DESTRUCT, SAME THING

The glow of Dolli and Julie's bodies was all that lit the halls of the lower dungeon while they walked the new section.

"Here's where I want to craft the hidden switchback," Julie said, pointing to a dead-end in the maze. She moved on, pointing to another wall feature as she talked.

Dolli followed, but her mind wandered. She needed to start making the hero quests to bring in allies, and she needed to break that news to Monster Haven soon. Heroes stood for everything evil and bad in their world, but Tina_Flamestorm, Katrina, gave her hope.

Not every hero was looking to steal and consume everything in Hafheim. Most of them seemed more like children, uncertain about the world and what was in it. They came from a world apart and didn't know Hafheim was *real*... It made hating them a little harder for Dolli.

"Overlord?" Julie asked.

"Uh, yes. This all sounds good," Dolli said.

"I asked if you were all right," Julie said and slowed to a stop.

"My apologies. You seem to have this under control, so my thoughts were elsewhere."

Julie chuckled. "Where's that?"

"Somewhere between Hafhaven and the void," Dolli mused, then shook her head. "Thank you for taking your responsibilities seriously."

"It's not just my home I'm protecting, it's Monster Haven, home to any peaceful monster trying to escape murderous heroes," Julie said.

Dolli sighed. "We need help, Julie, or we're not going to make it. We need heroes."

Julie recoiled and her body pulsed bright yellow. "Has all this been for nothin'? You've relied on them before, and *this* is where we got to!"

"We need more firepower and expendable troops. I've done the calculations. We'll last, at most, twenty-eight hours against his full force, which will be here in two days or less." Dolli picked up a pebble and tossed it down the dark corridor in frustration.

"What about finding another dungeon, makin' friends?"

Dolli shook her head. "How would we find them in time? How could they move in to save us in time? What if they have respawn restrictions inside our dungeon? There's too few dungeons around us, too far away, and at levels lower than ours. Heroes are a viable option. I can summon them directly into battle."

"But what if they turn on us?" Julie fluffed down beside Dolli and took her hands in hers. "We can't trust 'em."

Dolli was quiet.

"Is there nothing else we can do?"

Dolli shook her head. "There was one other thing I could think of. He likes to get close when he knows the end is near. I could use the dungeon core as a bomb to incapacitate him, blow a hole in his chest, and give you guys a chance to smash it."

"There's no other way?" Julie asked, picking up her own pebble and tossing it in futility.

Dolli shook her head. "I'd much prefer to turn *his* core into a bomb, but I don't think he'll let me fool around with his insides."

They sat in silence for a moment, then Dolli lifted from the ground. "We better get back to it."

"If you kill yourself, Monster Haven is done, right?"

"I think so. You'll be free to find another place of power and start fresh—maybe Greg could be your Overlord?"

Julie grimaced. "I've come to notice a few failin's in him that might not make the best leader. I'm glad you're our Overlord, Dollitrice."

"Thank you," Dolli whispered, then offered Julie a hand up.

"We better tell the others about this new plan."

"The suicide or the heroes?"

Julie snorted. "Aren't they both suicide?"

Dolli nodded. "Fair point."

She opened the Overlord menu and called for an officers' meeting. Everyone replied in chat, even Julie, that they'd be there.

"I need to drop heroes for a farming round. Start the tea, would you?" Dolli asked.

Julie nodded, and they parted ways.

Dolli made her way down to the open arena where she could summon the hapless heroes in for slaughter. She summoned in the first wave of twenty-five and provided minimal support from the back, electing to watch her dungeonfolk in action instead. They'd grown in skill and tactics over the weeks, and Dolli was proud of how well they were all adjusting.

She gave them a short break, then summoned the next round. This group was larger, nearly thirty heroes, and Dolli jumped into the fray. She used Burst of Speed to weave through the lines of tanks and dropped a Solstorm on their casters. Chaos ensued from there as the randomly collected heroes tried their best to organize against Dolli's troops.

"There's the leader!" someone shouted behind Dolli as she retreated to the safety of her Bronzite tanks.

A female hero charged, waving and shouting, "Hey, Dollitrice! What's up with this potion you're making?"

They were dying all around her, but more interested in

speaking with her than in saving their own lives? Dolli called for a hold on combat with just four heroes left, all in critical condition.

"What—" A hero coughed, sputtering gore onto his chest. He'd received too great a wound and his health bar emptied.

Dolli moved on to the next hero, the tank girl.

"What is this, then? Rumors spreading about us on *Rebit?*" Dolli asked in a critical voice.

The tank gave a bloody-toothed smile. "You know about Rebit? It's true then. You're... broken."

"What's the potion for?" another hero asked from the stranglehold of a muscled Osorath.

Dolli crossed her arms. "None of your business—yet."

"Yet?" The tank grinned wider. "Is this a new world event?"

"Oh muh gerd, I hope," the slowly strangling hero managed in gasps.

Dolli smirked. "Keep an eye on the Rebit, kids." She looked to her monsters and nodded. The heroes were ended in an instant, and with their demise came the notifications Dolli had been pining for. Dungeon level nine, and her own level up to sixteen.

[Congratulations – Your dungeon has reached Level 9]

Unused Monster Slots: [49/200]

Undistributed Roles: [1/7]

Open Lifestream Slots: [4/6]

Unclaimed Overlord Ability Points: [1]

[1] level remains until next dungeon ability: Modulate; Resolve.

Ascension Boost: The dungeon will now grow by 25 feet per level.

=====

Dolli opened the roles tab with hope swelling in her heart.

There was a new slot open, and that usually meant a new option was available, too. She almost shouted with joy when she saw what it was.

[Battle Commander]

The Battle Commander is a force to be reckoned with on the field. They can project their voice over the entire dungeon, set map pings, organize battalions, and use several abilities to command the troops.

It is recommended that the Overlord takes this role.

Oops, you've already assumed a role!

=====

While Dolli appreciated the system backhandedly chastising her for not being more patient for the "better role," she wasn't concerned. Battle Commander was *not* her style, but she did know just who to give it to.

She opened the chat menu and selected only Brene: *Meet in the cottage in five. Emergency.*

Brene couldn't reply—yet—but Dolli knew she'd be watching her notifications.

"Crawl the halls for stragglers. I'll be back with another round in half an hour," Dolli said to her troops, then bade them farewell.

She multitasked, wiggling along through the tunnels toward her cottage while she applied her stat points. She decided not to go with the usual configuration and dropped all five into Constitution. Having a few more Health points for her battle with Kelzoul would be welcomed.

[Dollitrice Grandmeir – Monster Character Sheet]

Name	Level	Alignment
Dollitrice Grandmeir	**16**	**Celestial**
Creature Type	Experience Points	Affiliation
Celestelle	**78**	**Monster Haven**
Health	Health Regen per sec	Carry Capacity LBS
680	**11.76**	**19.5**
Spark	Spark Regen per sec	Movement Speed Bonus
1500	**42.86**	**13%**
Agility	Constitution	Magical Affinity
12	**26**	**67**
Mental Prowess	Stamina	Strength
68	**18**	**5**
Melee Damage per sec	Ranged Damage per sec	Spell Damage
11.0	**26.4**	**149.6**
Crit Chance	Dodge Chance	Spell Crit Chance
7.00%	**11.55%**	**38.01%**
Armor Rating	Armor Piercing	Celestial Res.
15.50%	**8.50%**	**36.86%**
Divine Res.	Nature Res.	Nether Res.
43.88%	**29.84%**	**35.10%**

=====

As for her ability point, she decided to drop it in Fold Reality, another one of her most useful spells.

[Celestelle Ability: FOLD REALITY]

Spell type: Active

Cost: 150 Spark

Cast time: Instant

Cooldown: 5 minutes

Duration: 25 seconds

Range: 300 feet

Target: Any two points in space not occupied by a living being

Spark Alignment: Celestial

Description: Space is your domain, and you know how to bend the rules. Select any two points in space to be connected as if they were one.

Effects:

- Allow objects and Creatures to pass through each point in space as if they were the same point.
- Neither point can be cast on top of a living being* in a way that would bisect or otherwise trap them in the Fold.
- Any allies passing through the Fold will gain the Celestial buff "Reflect," increasing resistance to all spell types by 20% for 10 seconds.
- Any enemies passing through the Fold will gain the Celestial debuff "Repulse," adding a 15% chance to be stunned when physically attacked for 10 seconds.

*Disclaimer: Very small and microscopic beings are an exception.

======

The upgrade dropped the cooldown and increased the duration significantly, a huge boon. Not only that, but the buff and debuff for friends or enemies passing through the portal was a great addition.

All her officers, plus Brene, were waiting inside her home when she arrived. She pushed the door shut behind her and gave nods of recognition to everyone for coming.

"First order of business: Brene, I'd like to offer you the officer role of Battle Commander. It comes with interesting combat perks and the ability to send dungeon messages and map pings. It's a powerful and important job that we need done well."

Dolli pulled the Battle Commander pin from the ether of the menus and held it out to the towering Stagarth.

Brene dropped to a knee, but she was still a head above Dolli. She took the pin and pressed it to her chest. "I would be honored to serve Monster Haven in this way."

Dolli dismissed the notification that appeared for Brene's acceptance and watched as green light filled the room. The pin molded into Brene's chest, searing into her very being. The light in the pin dimmed, then thrummed in time with the others.

Julie clapped. "Well done!"

"Yes, welcome to the officer's team," Greg boomed. The hulking Bronzite was getting much too large for Dolli's table and chairs, but that was a logistical problem for another time.

Dolli sucked in a deep breath. "Now, for the reason you're all here—"

"Julie told us already," Rufus said.

"We support the decision to call in heroes to fight with us," Greg said.

Dolli scowled. "All of you?"

Nubiri growled. "I begrudgingly agreed. I would prefer my unborn child sssurvives."

The rest of the group nodded, even Brene. "I've been monitoring our power level through the Dungeon Information menu—just outside the cottage there." Brene pointed to the door to where Dolli assumed an access menu existed. "I compared this to the size of Kelzoul's army and used the monsters I fought against as a mid-level baseline for their overall strength."

Brene paused, uncertain, but Dolli nodded and she went on. "We don't have enough monsters at high enough levels. The dungeon itself needs to be three to six levels higher than it is to put up any kind of a fight against his forces. We'll need many disposable fighters to combat his style of endless waves. I assume this was the conclusion you came to hours ago, Overlord?"

"It was indeed," Dolli affirmed. She smirked at the pandering, or perhaps it was just courtesy that Brene was trying not to make her Overlord look bad.

"Good pick," Rufus whispered to Dolli with a wink and a nudge.

Brene's shoulders climbed up to her antlers and she shrank in on herself. She was beet red as she whispered, "Yes, well, the heroes would provide a near endless stream of forces to clash with Kelzoul's, if we can get them to agree not to kill *us*."

Greg crossed his arms and sat back, the little wooden chair whining under his weight. "We can't trust heroes not'ta do what's in their nature. They kill monsters and raid treasure holds," he said.

Dolli raised a finger. "This is where I've blundered in the past. The quest has explicit fail conditions I can fill in—though it does take a higher reward value. I can ensure they won't hurt the dungeonfolk of Monster Haven or raid our holds." At least, she hoped that was a condition she could set.

Rufus shrugged. "Not like we're using the mountains of coin we've collected from them."

"Ha, we'll be paying them with their own pilfered money. I like that," Greg said with smug satisfaction.

"We'll need to spread the word fast," Dolli said, opening her Hero Quest menu. She saw the simple quest she'd given to Katrina was completed, and she was online. Perfect.

"Get ready, everyone. Hero incoming."

CHAPTER THIRTEEN
THE ENDLESS RAID

"So, lemme get this straight. There's a wandering monster called Kelzoul who's amassed a huge army just to come eat your dungeon core?" Katrina asked, her eyes wide.

Dolli nodded, close enough.

Katrina scowled. "And you need me to post this quest to Rebit so you can build an army of heroes to throw against him until you can kill him?"

"Nailed it, as heroes say," Rufus said.

Katrina shook her head in disbelief, her grin wide. "This. Is. Awesomesauce! Yes of course I'll be the first ever Monster Haven Hero liaison!"

Greg held up a hand. "Bein' a little hasty with'at official title, aren't ya?"

Katrina bounced in her excitement. "Sure sure, no problem. Oh yeah, but I can't start until tomorrow. It's almost lights-out, and my mom will kick me out if I'm late for class again."

Dolli rested a hand on Katrina's shoulder, severity in her creased brow. "We'll be dead tomorrow."

She wasn't certain if that was true, but it was very possible. Kelzoul moved fast, and there was no doubt in Dolli's mind that he'd send ahead whatever Monster Haven defectors remained to begin the demoralization assault. She'd need heroes on the front lines to do that dirty work and keep her own dungeonfolk back deeper in the maze to spare them the mental anguish.

Katrina's smile faded. "You're serious?"

They all nodded solemnly.

"Sheet," the hero said, making the nonsense word sound like a curse.

"You're our only hope," Julie said, her hands pressed together in prayer. Her eyes were abnormally large and sparkly, her face molded into a pout. It was so convincing, even Dolli started to feel bad.

Katrina grimaced in frustration. "Damn. I really don't want you guys to die. Okay, I'll get some caffeine. Beer bee."

"What?" Boji asked, head tilted.

"Oh, it means I'll be right back." Katrina chuckled. Then her gaze went vacant and she sat up straight.

Dolli and the others watched the motionless mage for many long minutes.

"Is she… dead?" Greg asked.

Rufus poked her arm.

Katrina wobbled slightly on her chair, then returned to the upright position.

The mage leapt from the seat with a huge grin. "Alright, double-dutch espresso consumed. Let's do this thing!"

The monster cheers were interrupted by the door banging against the wall. An out-of-breath Toren knelt as soon as he saw the officers gathered. "Overlord, Kelzoul's troops have been spotted on the mountainside directly southeast."

Dolli took a deep breath. "Boji, I need you to start crafting some bombs. Tell me all the components you need in the chat."

"Right," he said with a dip of his head and dismissed himself.

"Greg, I need you to start crafting riding gear for Nubiri—" Dolli turned to look at the disgruntled wyvern. "With her consent to be ridden into battle with bombs strapped to her back?"

"There's little else choice," Nubiri grumbled.

"Good. At least three goblin riders across, and if you have time, work with Boji to make up a crossbow attachment for each side,"

Greg blew out his cheeks. "I'll see what I can manage."

"Rufus and Brene, get battle and rest rotations figured out. Julie, finish your in-progress builds and make a dead end out of anything that you can't." Dolli rapid fired the orders, whipping her officers into action.

Katrina cleared her throat. "And me, *Overlord*? What can your liaison do?"

"I need you to get these quests to every hero you can," Dolli said. The pair moved to the hearth to get out of the way of scrambling officers. Dolli scribbled out the first quest and passed it off to Katrina.

"Got it, thanks," she replied, then took a seat on Dolli's plush armchair.

"Hey, hey, Haf-timers!" Katrina said in a grandiose way. "It's me, your dopest of dungeon divers, Rexis Min on my alt Tina_Flamestorm."

"What are you doing?" Dolli asked as she watched the mage speak and gesture to thin air.

She whispered, "Oh, heh, I figured the fastest way to get word out was to go live. I've gotten fifteen *thousand* new subscribers since yesterday."

Katrina returned her attention to the air just above and in front of her. "That's right, everyone, I'm here with the Overlord of Chaos herself, Dollitrice Grandmeir!"

She flicked her hands through the air and looked at Dolli expectantly. "Say something," she whispered when Dolli stared back at her, dumbfounded.

Dolli waved to the thin air in front of Katrina.

The mage flicked her hands again and brought a big smile to her face. "We've got a special request tonight. You've seen her slaughter quests, her courier quests, and everything in between— except this!"

With a flourish of her hands, Katrina gestured to her left. Dolli's quest materialized in soft golden light. "We need any able-bodied hero ready to throw down for guts and glory to save the awesome Monster Haven Dungeon… for they are in dire straits."

The mage went on, talking to her "subscribers" about Monster Haven's horrible plight, and Dolli got back to business. In a few minutes' time, she'd made twenty nearly identical quests.

With the summoning quests completed, Dolli worked on the painstakingly complex "Battle for Monster Haven" quest. It outlined the rules of engagement, which included failure for any Monster Haven creature killed, among other things. This would hopefully disincentivize the murder of her own people.

With the restrictions piling up, the gold reward for the quest was up to one hundred and forty for *each* hero. That was fine, their treasury was full to the brim and as Rufus had said, they had no real need for the gold.

A chat notification appeared in the upper right of her vision and Dolli switched over. It was from Brene: *They're here. 1,000 out front, 100 or so preparing to enter the maze.*

Dolli: *We'll be down there soon for the first summon.*

"Katrina," Dolli said, interrupting the mage, who could talk nonstop.

"Wha?" The girl's head snapped in her direction.

"Want to give them a good look at the action?" Dolli asked with a cocky smile. One hundred enemies in the maze would be dispatched quickly, and what better way to whet the heroes' appetites than let them see how many monsters there were for the killing.

Katrina talked to her subscribers once more. "New development, the battle is kicking off. Let's go watch! Don't forget to donate to my VTube stream so I can keep going all night. You guys aren't gonna want to miss all this!"

Katrina jumped up and followed Dolli to the maze entrance. If it was true and there were fifteen thousand heroes watching her now, they could easily turn the tide of this battle.

She spared a glance at the hero quests and saw three were already taking on heroes, and one was almost at the limit. They needed to keep this influx coming steadily throughout the night, and Dolli had a brilliant idea how. Heroes loved four things: gold, loot, killing monsters, and competitions.

They had everything but the last bit. Dolli could fix that. "Any hero able to strike a crippling—but not killing—blow on Kelzoul will get two thousand gold and get to pick any one item from our treasure hoard."

Katrina had spun the imaginary view portal toward Dolli when she'd started speaking, then turned it back on herself with a gasp. "She is just straight *chaos!* What do you think, guys? Are you gonna sit on your ass and watch from VTube, or will you be rolling in the riches tomorrow?"

By the time they reached the middle levels, heroes were flooding into the quests. Three of them were full up, ready to go. Dolli had certainly picked the right *liaison.* While Dolli's offer was good, Katrina knew how to make it irresistible.

"Form up, heroes incoming." Dolli opened the quest menu and selected "Summon All." Her dungeonfolk raised weapons, but stayed back as the heroes materialized in golden sparkles.

The heroes unsheathed swords and readied spells, but didn't attack. She marked the quest complete for everyone, granting them a small amount of experience.

"Here is your new quest," Dolli said, then offered them "The Battle for Monster Haven."

The heroes went glossy-eyed as they reviewed the offer. Murmurs of "New content," "Cool world battle," and "Never seen this before" filled the crowd of heroes. Within seconds, they all accepted the new battle quest.

Brene stepped up beside Dolli. "Recruits! If you do not follow my directions in combat, you may kill one of our monsters. If you do that, you fail the quest. No reward, no more fun. We will turn on you faster than a pack of ravenous wolves. Understand?"

Some of the heroes whispered to one another, then a stout man in chainmail raised his axe. "So, you're like the raid leader?"

"I am your god down here," Brene said, confidence radiating off her in waves.

The heroes fell in line at Brene's commands, listening to her every word. "You may see some of our own in the enemy ranks—defectors. We will treat them just the same as the others."

"How will we know if it's you, or them?" a tall man in blue robes asked with his hand raised.

Brene turned to pace the line. "*We* will not attack you."

Another hero raised her hand. "When do we get our rewards?"

"When we've won," Dolli said. "Welcome to the endless raid."

CHAPTER FOURTEEN

BLUNDERS OF EPIC PROPORTIONS

The army of heroes and monsters marched side by side down to the bottom level. Every ramp they took along the outside provided a view of the battle awaiting them. Dolli stopped and looked through the window carved into the stone. The surviving defectors were there on the front line, trembling and terrified. Her heart broke for them. She had to do something.

"Whoa, and here's a view of what's to come, people," Katrina said, pulling up behind Dolli. "This is the single most epic world battle I've *ever* seen in Hafheim, and y'all are gonna miss it if you don't move your asses."

"Form up!" Brene called.

Dolli wiggled along through the crowd, getting to the front. She had one last thing she wanted to say. At the bottom of the dungeon, her defectors waited outside the entrance. Brene didn't leave her side as she stepped through the narrow doorway.

"We can win. Come back to us," Dolli said, her arms open to the defectors.

A coral-skin shouted from the middle of the defectors. "Kelzoul does not forget treachery!"

Katrina whispered from the doorway. "Look at this tense drama. Heart-wrenching."

"Come home!" Dolli called once more, and the defectors shifted in place, uncertainty in their terrified faces.

"For Haven!" a cry rang out from the enemy lines, and a sword ripped through the coral-skin's back, leaving a spray of red on the dirt behind him. The ogre creature stumbled, grasping at the hilt of the blade buried deep in his chest.

The defectors charged in all directions, ripping at the guards that escorted them.

"Help them!" Dolli called to the heroes at her back, and they charged forward.

"Coral-skins only!" Brene commanded, charging the enemy.

Dolli cast Zeal on her Battle Commander and she grew by three feet, towering over everything in her path. The Stagarth dropped her head and rammed into the crowd of Kelzoul's forces. Bodies flew from the force of her impact, and Dolli speared them with quick Spark Lances, ending them before they hit the ground.

The defectors ran toward Monster Haven, and a dozen join request notifications sprang into Dolli's view. A blue "Accept All" option appeared in the corner of her vision and Dolli smashed it without a thought. All at once, the red names of the defectors swapped to green.

Heroes and monsters battled side by side, coral-skins falling by the dozen.

"Fall back to Haven," Brene called when the slaughter ended. A semitransparent map appeared in the upper-left corner of Dolli's vision, and a red *ping* flashed at the door to the maze. Battle Commander abilities on display.

Dolli saw why she'd given the command. As the crowd of sword-slinging heroes dispersed, the second wave of Kelzoul's army could be seen charging forward.

This was the start of the *real* fight.

"Take up positions through the halls. Use the traps and block the tunnel when it's soon to be overrun. We want to funnel them into the drop zone!" Brene's voice carried through the group as if she were standing right next to Dolli, yet she was a good thirty feet behind her.

They crammed into the maze and spread through the side passages as ordered, Katrina close at Dolli's side. Dolli spared a moment to look at the quests. Three more full and two nearly there. This wasn't the pace of uptake she was hoping for, but they'd make it work.

The war cry of Kelzoul's army was like deadly music to their marching feet. Shielded monstrosities entered the maze two by two, blocking every physical attack thrown at them. Dolli dropped Gravity Well at the doorway, slowing down everything that came through and giving the heroes a fighting chance.

Brene bellowed commands and fired arrows from the center of the killing floor. Wispelles fired off heals and Zeals on the heroes while Oakenhearts buffed their strength. Bronzite and the newly transformed Ironhides blocked all attacks aimed at the casters in the back.

"This is so feckin' cool!" a hero called as they plunged their dagger into a shield-towering ogre's eyes. The monster dropped to his knees with a groan and disappeared in a puff of orange sparkles, returning to Kelzoul.

The bodies piled up at the entrance, then faded away in orange light. The obstructions, no matter how momentary, were welcome. The bright glow of the respawning enemies blinded the incoming forces, and the bodies tripped the running combatants, making them easy prey. Kelzoul's forces could barely get through before they were shot down by bolts of magic and sharp arrows.

"*Agah e'Ogish!*" bellowed a voice in the distance so loud and powerful it could've only been Kelzoul using his Battle Commander ability.

Not a second later, a message came through the chat from Brene: *Fliers to the tower walls, enemies climbing. Tanks, take a party of six ranged fighters to every window and provide support.*

Dolli followed a group of four to the next level, Katrina not far behind. From her vantage through the window, it looked like ants swarming a picnic. Wave after wave of battle-hardened monsters washed over the fields of wheat, trampling them into dust. Dolli watched in horror as the creatures leapt onto the base of her dungeon and scaled it easily with their claw-tipped hands and feet.

Noctaves sailed through the air, razor-sharp talons ripping monsters from the walls and tossing them back to the ground. Some hit the ground with bone-crunching snaps, then dissolved into orange, but others lay there and wailed in agony. Incoming monsters grabbed the critically injured by the head and ran sharp blades across their throats to end the screams.

Dolli recoiled at the ruthlessness. Monsters dying on the battlefield wasted time and resources, and Kelzoul knew this. Killing them and going to respawn was faster than dragging them back and repairing them. How cruel, and efficient.

"Mom, I can't pause. It's an *online* game!" Katrina yelled behind Dolli.

She turned to see the young mage staring vacantly toward the wall.

"This is serious! Please, another thirty minutes!" the mage whined.

A Noctave screamed and dropped through the air, three monsters hacking at its sides and legs with little blades. Dolli threw a Solstorm out the window, the golden light bouncing between her monster and the enemies in rapid succession. The enemies howled and convulsed, losing their grip on the avian assassin and falling to their death. The Noctave took back to the sky, its health bar below fifty percent but stable from Dolli's heal.

"Yes, I can stay!" Katrina said and rushed up to Dolli's side. "You guys, look at this *insane* battle. I keep telling you, you don't want to miss out on all this epicness. It's like LotR or something down here!"

A ping lit up Dolli's view, a message from Brene: *Need more heroes for the ground floor.*

She panned over to the quest menu and selected another of the full ones. She summoned all the heroes, and with her loudest voice, she commanded them downstairs to Brene. The heroes, giddy for murder, ran down to receive their assignments.

A ribbiting chorus of fire-belching eyeball monsters drew Dolli's attention back to the fight. Balls of flame arced across the distance from Kelzoul's back lines, only to land a few feet short in his own advancing troops.

Another war cry split the sky, this one loaded with fury. *"Yeh'gah!"*

The flying spheres of fire burps flapped their leathery bat wings and moved closer. Could that fire do serious structural damage to the tower? Dolli hadn't accounted for an assault on the dungeon itself, and she didn't want to wait around to find out.

She wrote a quick message to the Officer's chat: *Those fiery bastards need culling.*

A moment later, a flock of midnight blue Noctaves dove toward the enemy lines. In the fading light, Dolli saw silver flickering along the ground below the fire-belchers. It was a row of archers.

Dolli didn't have time to send a message. She leaned out the window and screamed, "Archers!"

A black mass on the outside wall of the tower caught her eye. It was an iron tube, corked with a fuse. Dolli's mind raced when she noticed another tube just five feet below it, and another one ten feet to the left.

She wrote another message to the officers in a flurry: *They planted bombs on the tower. They're going to bring it down on top of us!*

Brene's voice boomed over the battlefield. "Remove all foreign objects from the tower exterior! Bronzite, push through. Osorath, Noctaves, and Destratos, go get those bombs off Haven!"

The battlefield moved all at once, Kelzoul's monsters bearing down on the dungeon exit. They were going to block them in and blow them up. Dolli stared in horror, searching for a solution, anything to save them.

"*Fye!*" Kelzoul roared.

A horrible ribbit followed and fire streaked across the sky.

"Are they gonna blow us up?" Katrina asked.

"Seems as such," Dolli said, a plan forming in her mind.

She cast Gravity Well as far out as she could in the air. The incoming fireballs moved through the field and slowed, then dropped out of the sky onto the enemy horde at the foot of the tower.

Brene projected again a second later. "Wispelle, Gravity Well the incoming fireballs!"

Noctaves dived past the projectiles, blasting gusts of magical wind in their wake that pulled the attacks out of the sky. All around the tower, her people got creative, trying everything they could to stop the sparks that would light the fuse on the whole dungeon.

The first attack failed, not a single fireball getting through, but Kelzoul had an army of those regurgitative freaks in his arsenal. Another volley was already trailing toward Monster Haven.

Dolli's dungeonfolk climbed the outside of the tower, battling enemies as they removed the bombs. But her dungeonfolk were being overrun. It was a hundred to one down there, and Kelzoul's troops had encircled the tower.

A red notification flashed in Dolli's vision, and she opened the chat, opting to leave it up in the upper right corner of her vision.

Rufus: *Monster on the top level. We need heroes here.*

Brene: *Running thin down here.*

Dolli: *Sending fresh troops to you, Brene, and coming up to you, Rufus. We need to get these explosives out, now!*

A fireball blazed through the window next to Dolli and smashed into Katrina, knocking her back ten feet and searing her skin. Worried that it hadn't actually been aimed at them, Dolli leaned out the window to check on the three bombs nearby. Their fuses were sparkling.

She couldn't cast Fold Reality inside the wall, and she couldn't use Solstorm, Burst of Speed, Starfire, or any of the damn abilities she'd selected up to this point.

"Get down!" Dolli yelled, pulling her people back from the walls.

Katrina screamed in fury, half her health gone. She raised her staff and blue light burst from the crystal center and blossomed out in a shield around Dolli and the two closest dungeonfolk.

Time slowed to a crawl and a loud *boom* compressed the air around Dolli. The tower shook and chunks of rock blasted inward, smashing into her people's unguarded backs. The rocks shredded into sand against the Spark shield around Dolli.

A fist-sized rock smashed into Katrina's head, and she dropped her staff. The blue bubble around Dolli faded, and debris rained down around them. She pushed her people back toward the center compartment, then reached down for Katrina. Dolli's hand passed around and through Katrina's arm and she cursed.

Green moss grew across Katrina's chest, and a Stagarth down the hall yanked the unconscious mage out of the falling rock. Dolli wiggled along after her, barely evading the collapse. A large boulder smashed down against the hall as Dolli made it into the central room.

"Katrina?" Dolli asked the mage with concern. Her health bar was critically low.

"Did I help?" Katrina asked, her eyelids fluttering. Crimson trickled down her hair, matting it with the dirt of the tower.

"You saved me," Dolli said, removing a health potion from her inventory.

"No," Katrina said, putting a hand out to stop her. "You're going to need it."

"But you need it now. You're part of this fight!" Dolli urged.

Katrina smiled with bloody teeth. "My mom says I have to go, anyways. It's more heroic if I die in battle. Farewell, Hafheimers... see you at... respawn." Katrina's head dropped and she sighed out a last breath.

Dolli looked up to her frightened people. Their emotion

flowed through her like a river carves through a mountain. How could she stop this? How could she help the monsters trapped below?

Dolli looked down the hall to the dead-end, and then Julie flashed through her mind. *Then there's this hidden switchback.* The memory roared through her mind.

Dolli opened her chat, and as she spoke, she transmitted the message to the entire dungeon. "Everyone, make your way to the top level and remove as many of these explosives on the way as you can. Use the hidden exits Julie built into every level. All Stagarth and Oakenheart with Creeping Moss, start refilling your Spark now. I have a plan."

CHAPTER FIFTEEN

A GOD AMONG MONSTERS

D olli squeezed through and around the cracks in the rocks until she forced her way through the obstructions blocking the dungeon passages. When she emerged, she was met with a gaping hole in her tower that revealed waves of fire on the ground.

Kelzoul's army seemed endless in the deep twilight of her demise.

No. She could still beat him.

She turned away from the opening and used Burst of Speed, propelling herself through the maze. She zipped down crumbling passages until she heard the roars of combat on the ground floor. Dolli emerged at the last staircase to a bloody massacre. Brene was at the front, just outside the wide opening. She'd created a semicircle around the entry that allowed two dungeonfolk at a time to start scaling the walls.

Dolli charged forward and squeezed through to the front. "Relief is here!"

In a flash, Dolli summoned the second to last full quest of sixty heroes. "Guard our retreat!"

Brene called for the dungeonfolk to move back, and they ran. Dolli led them through the switchbacks around the blocked tunnels, and in a few, ground-trembling minutes, they'd reached the top.

Aerial troops clashed overhead in a shower of feathers and blood. Dolli and her monsters battled their way through the streets to the center of town. When they reached the X, Rufus was there waiting with the other Stagarths and Oakenheart.

Dolli hopped up on Rufus' shoulder and grabbed hold of his thorny antlers. She typed out a message, and read it aloud to everyone. "The tower is going down." She paused, her voice threatening to betray her. She started again, stronger, "But we can go down gently. We'll use Creeping Moss like a blanket to help contain the crumbling, dropping us to the ground while keeping the village safely balanced on top. Every Wispelle, find a Wendigo partner to cast Zeal on. Everyone else, keep them safe."

The dungeonfolk paired off chaotically, but quickly.

"What do we do once we're down?" someone asked from the crowd.

Dolli sucked in a breath. "He'll come to me to rub this defeat in my face and then we strike. We'll hit him hard with a hero summon, and he'll have to take the potion—and that will be the end of him. He'll be banished to Nevheröld for eternity."

There was murmuring and quiet sobs as the message sunk in. They were fighting for their very lives to the last dungeonfolk.

Dolli looked down at Rufus and whispered, "Do you think this is going to work?"

"I hope so," he said quietly.

"I'm so sorry if it doesn't." Dolli swallowed back the feeling of tears, though she couldn't cry in her vapor form.

"It's been a wild time," Rufus said somberly, then smirked. "We still might beat him, you know."

Dolli chuckled. "Right. I've been doing the math, you see—"

"Don't tell me the odds," Brene interrupted. She grinned deviously and said, "It'll spoil the thrill of battle."

Resolve coursed through Dolli. She couldn't condemn them with her mind before the battle had been decided. They still had a chance, and Dolli was going to do everything in her power to make the most of it.

The rumbling underfoot grew, and Dolli knew it was time.

"Creeping Moss and Zeal at the ready!" Brene yelled over the whole dungeon.

"We're protecting special cargo," Dolli said, pointing to her cottage.

Rufus knew right away what she meant. Not only was the dungeon core under Dolli's home, but Nubiri's last baby was roosting by the augmented chimney. Rufus sprinted on all fours toward the cottage, and Brene boomed a countdown.

"Ten, nine, eight…"

The tower rumbled but the roads held together. Rufus skidded to a halt and pressed his palms against the wood of Dolli's home.

"Three, two, one!"

Dolli buffed Rufus with Zeal and he grew by several feet. Thick green moss spread from his hands across the cottage and around Nubiri's egg, then down across the road. His moss connected with that of another Wendigo, and the spells interlocked. The green rolled over the village and cascaded down the edges, wrapping their homes in safety.

By the gods, it was working!

The ground shook and the tower tilted, finally giving way under the constant assault. Stone crumbled at the gaping holes left by explosions, and the village section slammed down into the lower half. Maze rooms collapsed, sending off notifications in Dolli's view about the critical damage to her dungeon.

"Hold!" Brene yelled above the grinding roar of boulders smashing into the ground. Dirt plumed up all around the village as they fell seventy feet. The stomach-turning sensation of gravity lessening filled Dolli's stomach, knotting it a hundred times over with the fear of her people.

They hit another section hard, jostling nearly everyone to their knees. But the Creeping Moss held them together. A cloud of brown dust rushed up and domed over the village and they slowed to a stop.

Dolli waved her hand in front of her face to clear the dust, but it persisted.

"Did we do it?" Rufus asked, then coughed.

"I think so." Dolli used Burst of Speed to get up on the roof of her cottage, then zipped across the distance to an open window on the X. She floated up the stairs and pushed out onto the roof, above the thickest part of the dust.

Rocks tumbled and slipped down the edges of the hill of rubble, now spread out several hundred feet in all directions but only thirty or so feet high compared to its once ninety. Queasy desolation bloomed in Dolli's gut as she looked on the ruins of their home and what lay beyond them.

Orange even brighter than the sun lit up the sky as thousands of Kelzoul's soldiers returned to him for respawn. The glowing light didn't go far, collapsing in on a single point just a few hundred feet from Dolli. A sea of coral-skinned creatures swarmed around the rubble but parted at his coming.

It was time to gloat.

Dolli jumped down onto Rufus' shoulder. "He's coming."

She opened her quest menu and looked at the full roster quest. It was the last one left.

"Witch in her castle, now ghoul to ruins!" Kelzoul roared. He was still a good hundred feet from the city's edge, but loud as can be. It shook the hearts of her people to know death was so close, and that rattle battered her fading hope.

No, this was still part of the plan. They had a chance.

Dolli sighed. "Let's go crush this bastard."

Rufus puffed up his chest and stalked to the center of town. He stopped next to Brene and the other dungeonfolk, bringing an air of confidence with him that lifted their spirits. An icon appeared in the corner of Dolli's vision, and she spared a glance at the buff.

[Lieutenant's Last Stand]

At the brink of ruin, the Lieutenant will bring you a final hope in the form of strength to defeat your enemies and defend your home.

Effects:

- +10 Strength
- +20 Constitution
- +5 Agility
- +10 Magical Affinity
- +15 Mental Prowess
- +15% Spark Regeneration while in combat

Duration: 15 minutes.

======

Dolli whispered to Rufus, "Holding out on us this whole time?"

"I figured now's sort of the last chance. Three-day cooldown," he said.

Through the settling dust Dolli could see the orange-glowing Overlord. He'd grown nearly a foot since she'd last seen him, and his muscles bulged beyond reason. The fleeting jovial moment faded, replaced with determination. No matter how big he got, Dolli and her dungeonfolk would not give up, and they wouldn't fail.

The orange light swirled and pulled around Kelzoul as if it were trying to escape him. He sucked down a deep breath, and the light fell into him like shooting stars. His muscles rippled and he grew another half-foot in size. His "guard" was now only half his height, looking like children next to Kelzoul.

"You thought you knew every… little… thing… didn't you?"

Kelzoul asked, stopping just twenty feet from where Dolli sat on Rufus' shoulder.

Dolli opened the quest menu in half her vision, multitasking while her thoughts hovered over the "Summon All" button. "I could say the same thing about you."

Kelzoul laughed. "You're defeated! What's more to know?"

Dolli hopped down, nodding for the others to back up.

"Now you want to challenge me to a duel?" Kelzoul asked, an amused glint in his wild, orange-glowing eyes.

His body looked as if the light would rip a hole through his skin at any second. His muscles twitched and flexed in seemingly uncontrolled ways, giving Kelzoul fear-inducing tremors. He was itching to fight—no, to slaughter.

"I think there's a great many things you didn't account for," Dolli taunted.

Kelzoul lifted his hand and Dolli tensed, but waited. He produced something from his inventory with a glimmering flourish: a potion.

"You mean this?" he asked, holding Dolli's poison to the sky.

Dolli's wide-eyed gaze betrayed her, making Kelzoul grin like a vulture. He uncorked the bottle and turned its contents out, splattering them on the ground.

Hopelessness washed over Dolli, turning her icy cold.

"Of all your failures, I will cherish this most." Kelzoul charged forward, and Dolli's mind flickered to the button.

In a blinding flash, sixty heroes materialized between her and the maniacal overlord.

"Kill that monster!" Brene commanded, and everyone snapped into action.

Magic bolts flashed and swords clashed, pushing Kelzoul back. He struggled to gain his footing, losing sight of Dolli in the crowd. He smashed through the first hero tank, then used their body like a club to beat the others back. Starfires roared and Bronzite fists crashed as the battle resumed all around them.

Nubiri swooped from the sky like a demon, the goblin on her

right shoulder belching fire from the nozzle of a massive turret while the goblin on her left unloaded wicked crossbow bolts into Kelzoul's guards. The enemy line fell back, leaving Kelzoul stranded with his three generals in a ring of heroes.

But it was all for naught if Dolli couldn't get some of that potion in him. Or, what if she could get it *on* him? Perhaps not the same effect as consuming it, but she was willing to try any option they had left.

"Knock him into the air!" Dolli yelled, the perfect plan hatching in her mind.

The heroes swarmed around Kelzoul, all trying to get a piece of him. This wouldn't work if she couldn't get a clear shot at him. She couldn't cast her second portal if any living creature bisected it.

"Nubiri! Grab and toss!" Brene bellowed the command.

The wyvern banked, coming around to snatch the overlord. They would only get one real shot at this.

Dolli locked eyes with the wyvern and prepared the first portal over the puddle of potion next to her. Nubiri's clawed feet dipped down into the crowd and locked on Kelzoul's oversized shoulders. The wyvern flapped her wings hard and turned up, throwing the overlord with all her weight.

Nubiri went down hard, the force of throwing the massive overlord too much for her to keep to the sky. She skidded across the road and slammed into the X, loosing the goblin saddle from her shoulders and spewing fire into the building.

Dolli tracked Kelzoul's path through the air, placing the second portal right where it needed to be. He fell through the invisible opening and dropped directly into the pool of poison he'd so carelessly dumped.

Dolli's heart stopped as the liquid smeared across his arms and face. The overlord rolled to his side with a roar and climbed to his feet. She held her breath, begging all the gods for help. *Let this be his end*, she whispered in her mind.

"You think magic tricks will stop me?" He whirled until he

found Dolli. He leered, his bloodlust intensified. But then, a bright rip pulled across his bicep like a zipper, spilling orange ooze down his arm. Kelzoul winced, then poked the liquid with a curious swipe of his finger.

Another tear burst across his chest, orange goop spraying on his armor. Kelzoul roared in anger and charged Dolli. She turned tail with Burst of Speed, zipping around the legs of stampeding heroes.

"You won't escape!" Kelzoul bellowed with an unnatural growl. Dolli looked over her shoulder to see the overlord gaining on her, and gaining in size. The orange oozing down his arms and legs twisted and pulled his body out of proportion until Kelzoul was nearly fifteen feet tall.

The mad overlord screamed in pain, dropping to the ground with a thud. Dolli stopped and stood her ground. The madman looked up, his eyes bloodshot and swollen.

"You've miscalculated again," he said through gritted teeth. "And now you'll all pay the price."

The orange leaking from Kelzoul's body slurped back into him, and he flexed out a bright shock wave in all directions. "Now you *all* will pay!"

Kelzoul's officers crumpled to their knees, orange light ripping out through their eyes, nose, and mouth. The glowing respawn essence flashed through the air and smashed into Kelzoul, making him grow. Another orange beam fired through the air and hit the Overlord, bulking him.

"What's happening to him?" a dungeonfolk cried.

"He's entering his final form!" a hero yelled with glee.

Dolli pulled a Spark potion from her inventory and downed it, then wiped her mouth with her wispy arm. "Get ready for the boss battle of your lives, noobs!"

CHAPTER SIXTEEN

KAIJU COMBAT

Kelzoul's skin tore, and clothes pulled apart as he stretched beyond his limits. The battlefield was alight with respawn essence as Kelzoul's army disintegrated, fueling him. The overlord mutated, trying desperately to hold his wretched bones together. He was thirty feet tall and still growing, the seemingly endless supply of monsters in his army dying to mutate him. He twisted and stretched toward the sky, roaring with pained madness.

Dolli knew that his army would be used up soon, and they'd have to battle him once more. She looked over the remaining ten or so heroes and her battered dungeon troops. She opened her quest menu and scrolled through the barren list. They were all empty, save one: Plague in the Crossroads.

There had to be an option left to them. Dolli opened her dungeon menu, the XP bar jumping out at her. They were just a few hundred XP short of leveling up to 10. Dolli flipped over to the dungeon abilities and read the text at the bottom of the Modulate ability.

"The dungeon will reshape itself to fight *any* threat," she whispered, then looked at the heroes.

She opened her chat menu and sent a dungeon-wide message: *Kill the heroes.*

Dolli closed the menu and looked to her puzzled dungeonfolk. There was a beat of confusion, and then action. Brene was first to strike, spearing the closest robed hero through the back with her powerful antlers.

"What the fuu—" a hero screamed out but was cut short by Dolli's Spark Lance.

"They're turnin' on us!" Another hero tried to raise the alarm but it was too late, the dungeonfolk descended on them with savagery.

In moments, the heroes were slain and all that remained was Monster Haven and Kelzoul. The orange light pouring into him slowed and so did his growth. The pain lessened in his roars, and he was coming to.

Dolli opened her menu and cursed. They needed five more XP. *Five!*

Keegan.

Dolli opened the quest menu and crossed her fingers. The summon button was selectable.

"Yes!" Dolli cried out and summoned the last hero they'd need.

Keegan appeared in a blur of golden light, then stared straight up at Kelzoul. "Oh sheet." He whirled around to find Dolli staring him down. His face sank from horror to desolation. "Oh, sheet."

"Thank you for your sacrifice," Dolli said and speared him through. The monsters stabbed, hammered, punched, and beat Keegan to death, giving the dungeon the final XP needed to level up. Dolli opened the dungeon menu and went to the abilities with a thought, then selected Modulate.

Kelzoul staggered back, then shook his head as his senses seemed to return to him. He picked up a giant foot and aimed it right at Dolli. With a final prayer to the gods for strength and luck, Dolli activated the new ability.

The ground trembled and the Creeping Moss flexed around

the stones of the destroyed Haven. In a blink, a shimmering opalescent dome formed over the center of town, protecting Dolli and her people. Kelzoul's foot slammed down on the crystal shield. The sound was louder than thunder, but the dome held fast against the attack. Kelzoul stepped back, then launched a powerful punch at the dome. The boom shook people to the core, and a crack formed in the top.

The ground rumbled again and the stones lifted, shifted, and locked into place. They rose from the ground in four massive, stumbling steps like a horse rising to its feet for the first time. The stony head of a turtle covered in moss snapped from the ground and caught Kelzoul's next attack in its sharp beak.

The monstrous overlord cried out in pain, then ripped his hand away, spraying orange goop across the solid dome. But that didn't stop him. He lifted another foot to smash down on the shield, and Dolli swore she heard him bellow her name in his war cry.

Thunderous booms rang out overhead followed by another crack in the shield, this one opening a wide hole. She couldn't wait for the dungeon to fight this battle itself—they had to help. But how?

The dungeon turtle snapped its head out like lightning and latched on to Kelzoul's offending leg. There was a loud *snap* and the bone in Kelzoul's leg broke under the pressure of the dungeon's bite. Orangey goop dribbled down his leg, but the wound was already on the mend. Kelzoul limped forward to deliver another punch to the turtle dungeon.

A chill swirled through the open hole at the top of the dome, and snow fell all around them. A hollow-belled jingle and a "Ho, ho, ho" filled Dolli with unexpected hope. Taffy and his posse galloped through the opening at the top of the turtle's frosty shell, then landed and slowed to a trot before Dolli.

"Looks like you found the ultimate shit-your-pants ability!" Taffy said. He dismounted and stood next to Dolli. "Need some help?"

"I thought you said we didn't have a chance?" Dolli asked.

He shook his head. "Nah, I said your chances were *bad*, but not zero. How we fightin' this creep?"

Dolli looked around the wreckage of her home. Bits of undetonated dynamite sat amid the crushed and mossy stones, and a plan started taking shape in Dolli's mind.

"Taffy, you said Kelzoul's dungeon core was inside him somewhere, right?"

The elf nodded. "His chest, well protected by thick ribs."

"Compromised ribs," Dolli said with a gleam in her eyes. "That turtle just snapped his femur, one of the strongest bones in the body. I have no doubt we can get past a few ribs."

Dolli waved Brene over to be her amplifier. The Stagarth projected Dolli's commands across the entire dungeon.

"Get the turrets outside the shell. We're going to attach bombs to the ballistae bolts and aim for the chest. Boji, craft a special bomb I can attach a potion to, preferably with a long wick. Greg, craft more bolts for the ballistae. Brene, get fighters out there to man the weapons and healers to keep them from dying. Rufus, get everyone who can't fight to help Boji or Greg."

Dolli stopped for a much-needed deep breath. "For Haven!"

The dungeonfolk echoed her war cry with determination she could feel. This wasn't over yet.

Dolli turned to Taffy. "Have any skill in alchemy?"

"Doll, I've been brewin' potions since before you were born," Taffy said with a cocky smirk.

Dolli took off for her alchemy lab. "What kind of potions can you make?"

"The kind that puts hair on your chest."

Dolli whirled on him. "You mean you're a brewer? That's not the same."

"Hey, I'm not just a brewer. I'm a master-level distiller."

Dolli rolled her eyes and pushed open the dilapidated door to her alchemy lab. It wasn't as bad on the inside as it was on the outside, but it was still in disarray, and Dolli worried it would take too long to find everything she needed. If only the dungeon knew the alchemy lab was key to surviving the threat, perhaps it could reshape—

Magical green Spark lit up the room. The light was blinding for a second, and Taffy yelped in surprise, shielding his eyes. Debris melted into the floor and tables, shelves repaired themselves, and jars of ingredients disappeared, then rematerialized in their proper place. Dolli watched it all in awe as the dungeon repaired her lab.

"Wow, that was somethin'," Taffy said.

"No time to gawk. We have a dungeon to kill."

Dolli used her Vapor Form ability to take a human, solid shape. Her feet dropped to the floor, and the trembling of the ground pulled her into the moment. She moved to the shelves with purpose, reaching out for vials, jars of herbs, tongs, and more. Taffy followed behind, taking everything from her and setting it on the clean workstation.

Dolli paused. "I need you to handle the final product."

"Why?" Taffy looked concerned, as if Dolli had tricked him.

"If my Spark touches it, we might all blow up."

"Might?" he asked, voice raised with tension.

"The potion will have a high-energy reaction with material from the Lifestream, and since I'm directly connected to the dungeon core—which has Lifestream energy flowing through it—it's possible."

Dolli watched as the plan clicked into place for Taffy. "You're gonna blow up his core."

"Hopefully."

Taffy smiled. "Then let's get to work."

CHAPTER SEVENTEEN

DUNGEON DIVEBOMB

"Carefully," Dolli said, watching Taffy pour the two cocktails together into the jar for the final potion.

"Have some faith. I don't intend to mess up when my life's on the line."

Steam rolled out of the top of the jar as the fluids mixed. Dolli pulled up her rubber apron and stepped back, not wanting any of it to touch her. The alchemy lab trembled but Taffy kept his footing. Not a drop spilled.

"Now, put in the final ingredient. You'll have to cork it *immediately*."

Taffy glanced over his shoulder with a raised brow. "I've got this, alright? I won't let you down."

The green potion whipped about, unstable. Taffy lined up the dropper of sparkling gold liquid over the opening with one hand and held the cork in the other. A single golden drop fell into the green liquid and Taffy slammed the cork home with a squeak. The green potion swirled into purple, with effervescent bubbles forming on top that tried to escape.

Taffy gave the bottle a little twirl in his palm, then handed it over to Dolli. "What'd I tell ya? Am I good, or am I good?"

"You're lucky, and somewhat skilled." Dolli stored the potion in her inventory and headed toward Boji's tinkering shop.

Kelzoul raged outside the cracked dome, throwing wild punches and kicks that the dungeon was getting surprisingly good at blocking for just being a turtle. The moss-covered beak of the turtle's head caught kicks and deflected punches with its own quick and powerful strikes—though it was only on the defensive.

The dungeonfolk had taken over offence, blasting holes in Kelzoul's chest that were healing slower and slower, which meant good news for Dolli. He was running out of energy, and hopefully his resulting explosion wouldn't level her village.

Boji was at the center of his shop, eyes down and mind engrossed in his work when Dolli came in.

"Ready yet?" she asked, rushing to his side.

"Moment longer," he whispered, delicately twisting a tiny screw on the side of a strap. It looked to be a cage for the potion.

"There," he said and set the tool aside, then opened his hand to Dolli. She placed the potion, their one chance, in his grasp.

He pulled the straps around the bottle and twisted the gears at each cross, retracting the leather and tightening the cage. Boji pointed to a dial and a switch at the top. "Sixty seconds, thirty seconds, no seconds," he said, pointing to the hastily carved hash marks around the dial. "Switch starts time. Switch can't be undone. Get it?"

"I've got it," Dolli said, reaching for the bomb.

Boji passed it to her, then placed his other hand on her shoulder. "Be careful, Overlord."

"We will," Taffy said, putting his hand on Dolli's other shoulder.

Dolli nodded to Boji with a quick thanks, then rushed out to the street.

"Who said anything about *we*?" she asked Taffy.

"How'd ya plan to get it in there?" Taffy spread his arms out wide and puffed up his cheeks. "Bastard's huge."

Dolli scowled.

Taffy grinned. "Oh boy, hadn't thought of that step yet, had ya?"

Dolli furrowed her brow. "I most certainly had. Nubiri will take me."

She opened the dungeon troops menu to see Nubiri's monster card grayed out; she was waiting in line for a Lifewell spot. There wasn't a Noctave left, and not a single other creature in the dungeon that could fly—reliably. Dolli cursed.

"How 'bout it, Doll, need another flier for your army of monsters?" Taffy asked, and a pop-up appeared in her vision.

[Taffy Milkfroth and his Ex-Mas Posse want to join Monster Haven!]

Taffy speaks for his band of elves and reindeer known as [Ex-Mas Posse], offering to join forces with your dungeon, [Monster Haven].

The Elves		The Reindeer	
Taffy Milkfroth	[Accept? Y / N]	Roodaulf Crimson Whiffer	[Accept? Y / N]
Peppermint Chewie	[Accept? Y / N]	Dancier Pirouette	[Accept? Y / N]
Truffle Tribble Trout	[Accept? Y / N]	Dixen Godrender	[Accept? Y / N]
Ginger Bier	[Accept? Y / N]	Slasher Hashslinger	[Accept? Y / N]
Caramel Driztel	[Accept? Y / N]	Comette Longtail	[Accept? Y / N]
Cookie Crumbie	[Accept? Y / N]	Clupit Piterpatter Clopit	[Accept? Y / N]
Eggnog Slipslurpor	[Accept? Y / N]	Gonner Frieunden	[Accept? Y / N]
Fudge Leiberwie	[Accept? Y / N]	Lancer Ace DeLume	[Accept? Y / N]
Gumdrop Sprinkle	[Accept? Y / N]	Mitzen Mörder	[Accept? Y / N]
[Accept All]		[Decline All]	

=====

"Are those really your full names?" Dolli asked, unable to contain her laugh.

Taffy went red in the face. "Fine, I'll just redact the offer!"

"No! It's a great name. Very great. But seriously, what's going on with Dixen Godrender?"

Taffy smirked. "You'll have to ask her about it sometime."

"I think I will," she said, and accepted the Ex-Mas Posse.

Green mist swirled from Dolli into the elf. The name over his head shifted from gray to green, matching Dolli's dungeon essence.

She smiled. "Welcome to Monster Haven."

"Hey, thanks." Taffy grinned back. He turned and whistled for his reindeer. The towering brown beast galloped down the road and skidded to a stop before Taffy. Roodaulf lowered his head until Taffy could reach its antlers and pull himself up.

He turned and reached back for Dolli. "So, needin' that ride?"

Dolli solidified her body and grasped his hand, then climbed onto the back of the reindeer. Taffy leaned down and whispered something in the beast's ear, who clopped his hoofed foot to the ground and bobbed his head in reply.

The elf whooped loudly. "Let's go kick some ex-overlord ass!"

Nine reindeer with their elven riders lifted off from the streets of Monster Haven, each with an additional ranged attacker on their backs. Dolli looked around in confusion.

"You coordinated all this?" she yelled to Taffy.

He seesawed his head. "Eh, kinda. Well, it was mostly your general, Brene."

Dolli opened her menu to see a host of messages Brene had sent dungeon-wide. Dolli had become so caught up in the potion crafting that she'd completely missed all of them. But Taffy couldn't have seen those until he joined the dungeon.

She closed the menu and leaned in to yell at Taffy again. "How did you know?"

Taffy tapped his temple. "Elven secrets!"

"Telepathy?" Dolli asked. That would explain how they'd communicated with just glances before.

"Smart, pretty, and overlord of your own dungeon. Only weakness: legs!" Taffy laughed. "Don't worry, Doll, we can be your wings."

Dolli withheld her groan. The elf was laying it on thick at such a time—he must've been all nerves under that confident façade.

They swooped low to pick up speed, then turned straight up through the crack in the dungeon dome. It was hard to see anything in the darkness but Kelzoul's glowing orange blood dripping from his mended wounds. He healed so quickly, their damage had already been undone.

Kelzoul swiped a massive hand toward the top of the shell, and Roodaulf bleated fearfully. Dolli cast Gravity Well, hoping part of him would be trapped by it and slow the rest down.

Kelzoul's massive hand decelerated just before impact, and the reindeer brigade slipped through the gaps in his fingers. Roodaulf kicked off the back of the oversized knuckles and turned toward the Overlord's chest.

Brene's voice boomed across the dungeon as she said, "Prepare to fire!"

"I'll kill you!" Kelzoul shouted, his words rattling the sky.

His other hand dropped from overhead, aiming to squash Dolli onto the dome. The turtle lunged, snapping its rocky beak around the overlord kaiju's wrist just above their heads, and Dolli felt a rush of air whoosh past her.

"Hold on!" Taffy yelled, and Dolli grabbed his sides tighter.

The reindeer flipped in one powerful leap, landing upside down onto Kelzoul's hand. They followed the lines of the giant's bones to his elbow, then turned toward his bicep.

"Fire all!" Brene cried.

Sparking ballistae whistled through the air and slammed into Kelzoul's ribs. With a series of juicy pops, Kelzoul's chest blasted open, spraying orange over the turtle's shell.

Dolli couldn't see the dungeon core inside the Overlord's chest, but there were… tunnels? Ghostly animas wandered from side to side in the wide opening, watching Dolli and the reindeer approach with bloodlust.

Had Kelzoul been physically transformed into a dungeon?

"Ready to get messy?" Taffy asked.

Dolli held her breath and nodded.

Roodaulf leapt from the monster's bicep and soared into the quickly closing hole in the Overlord's chest. Taffy fired three arrows faster than Dolli could register, but the magical shots passed straight through the waiting ghosts at the tunnel's entrance.

Dolli fired off a Divine aligned Spark Lance that impaled the first ghastly creature to the living wall of Kelzoul's chest. Roodaulf's feet squished and sprayed orange over the stretched sinew of Kelzoul's body. The ghosts descended on the few reindeer that made it inside, but the other Wispelle were quick to follow Dolli's lead with Divine Spark Lances.

"Where do we go?" Julie asked.

"Deeper," Dolli said, urging Taffy forward. "The ghosts will be trying to respawn—follow them!"

Roodaulf trotted through the low-ceilinged dungeon, his head dipped so Dolli could fire rounds of Spark at the attacking ghouls. The deeper they went, the louder Kelzoul's pounding heart and the cries of his murdered dungeonfolk became. Dolli cursed herself for every Spark Lance, knowing with every hit she landed, that creature might never respawn.

If she succeeded, none of them would ever respawn…

That was the price that had to be paid now, to save Hafheim from Kelzoul's reign.

The squad galloped through the tunnels, winding their way into Kelzoul as they followed the density of spirits to his core until they came to a thick sea of essence. Orange shades of the creatures they once were reached toward the glowing mass at the center of a large cavern, begging for respawn.

The crystalline dungeon core was strung up by strands of flesh, well out of reach of the ghouls. Dolli looked on the masses with pity, and then her heart broke. There was Henrietta the Oakenheart, grasping, pleading, wailing for life. She couldn't give it to her.

But she could give them all peace.

"Get me up there," Dolli told Taffy.

"There's not enough space to take off," Taffy said as the bodies pressed in around them.

The Wispelle in the back fired shot after shot to keep them

clear, and Dolli knew they would run out of Spark soon. They had to finish it.

"Give me an arrow and string."

Taffy pulled one from his quiver and ripped the jingle-less string of bells from his boot. Dolli pulled the dungeon-ending bomb from her inventory and cranked the dial to sixty, then wrapped the arrow to it tightly.

"We have sixty seconds, get going!" she yelled at the others.

"Get back!" Taffy echoed, and his elven posse responded, turning around.

The horde was closing in, their dead eyes begging Dolli for help. She flipped the switch on the bomb, then cast Fold Reality over the skin supporting the dungeon core. She stabbed the arrow through the portal. The bomb imbedded in the flesh securely, and the cavern trembled.

A deafening rumble shook all around them as Kelzoul cried out, "Kill!"

The ghouls charged Dolli and Taffy, rage in their once desperate eyes.

"Hang on!"

Roodaulf reared up and kicked at the ghouls with blue-glowing hooves, then turned and ran back the way they came. Dolli downed a Spark potion and turned to protect their retreat. The spirits tripped and trampled over one another, trying to get at Dolli.

"Kill!" The deep rumble of Kelzoul's angry voice shook the fleshy orange walls around them, urging the ghosts on.

"Ah, just shut up and die, fartbag!" Taffy shouted.

They twisted and turned through the squishy halls, an avalanche of angry spirits tumbling after them.

"It's blocked!" someone cried from the front where Kelzoul's chest was freshly mended.

"Then we'll make a hole!" Julie replied, pulling dynamite from her inventory.

Dolli twisted all the way around on Roodaulf, ready to unleash every spell in her arsenal. The ghouls weren't far behind. She had to give them time to escape. Two glowing arrows whizzed past Dolli's head and imbedded in opposite walls behind them. They exploded in a shower of white, and an icy barrier spread across the opening.

The spirits piled against the other side, banging goopy orange fists on the transparent obstruction. The dynamite detonated, blasting Dolli from the back of Roodaulf and shattering the icy wall. The spirits shook their heads, disoriented, and Dolli rushed to the front.

Cool wind from the outside blew in from a hole too small for anyone to escape through.

"Hope you've got one more trick up your sleeve!" Taffy said, fear showing in his trembling hand as he fired another volley of ice arrows at the ghouls. Every shot froze a monstrous body in place, but that didn't stop the horde. They charged forward, smashing into frozen spirits and scattering their pieces across the oozing floor.

Dolli looked back to the shrinking opening. Not everyone had to escape, just her.

Dolli put her hand on Taffy's shoulder. "One last trick. Die for me?"

Taffy's eyes went wide with fear, but he nodded. "Clear a path!"

Dolli rushed past the panicking reindeer and icy arrows fired by elves. The shades clamored after her, trying desperately to keep Dolli inside, in the blast radius, where her destruction would be assured alongside Kelzoul's.

Julie pummeled the coming horde with Divine Spark Lances, yelling, "Go, Dolli, go," with a death-ready grin. She stepped in the path of the horde when Dolli passed, ensuring her escape.

Dolli leapt from the ground and compressed herself into the shape of a tiny wyvern, then fired Burst of Speed. She squeezed through the goopy opening into the night air and turned down to pick up speed. Kelzoul screamed, the agony of failure and impending destruction carried in his voice.

Bright white light erupted from behind Dolli. Whether she or her dungeon lived didn't matter now. Kelzoul was destroyed. He could bring this terror to no other dungeon or village. They'd saved their realm from his plague. And that was enough.

The shock wave slammed into Dolli's wings, and they buckled under the strain. The turtle head reached out with its mouth open wide, reaching for Dolli. She had no other way to escape the blast that burned her back raw, so she soared into the turtle's mouth. She plunged through the tunnel, praying one last time for her people as blackness consumed her vision.

GODS REST, DUNGEONS ROAM

Dolli opened her eyes. Had she fallen asleep? She was in a cave, and the sun was rising outside. A thunderous boom shook the floor and Dolli jumped up, fully alert. Then it all came rushing back to her: Kelzoul, the explosion, the turtle dungeon snapping her up. She was still in its mouth.

Another vibration shook the cave with a low singsong wail, blowing air out the turtle's beak. Dolli leaned down, patting the rocky tongue of the turtle.

"Think you could put me up on your shell?" she asked, hoping the turtle could both hear and understand her.

A strong sense *protecting* flowed through Dolli, and the turtle's mouth closed a small measure. It vocalized again, and Dolli could feel the intention. She was safe in his mouth.

Dolli went to the edge and looked out. They'd moved a good deal away from where they had battled Kelzoul. The charred, steaming mass of his remains could be seen on the horizon, but the turtle dungeon was stationary now.

"You protected us well... What's your name?" Dolli asked, uncertain if she'd get a reply.

Images of different large, mossy stones flashed through Dolli's mind.

"Stony?"

The turtle clicked in disagreement.

"Boulder?"

Another rejection.

"How about Fjaar? It means 'strength of the mountain' in my old tongue," Dolli offered.

The turtle singsong moaned, pleased with the selection.

"Good. Well, Fjaar, I need to return to the city. I'll be safe there too," Dolli said in a soothing voice.

Fjaar clicked deep in his throat, then the view outside his mouth shifted. They moved until Dolli could see the edge of his shell, and the weapons her dungeonfolk had mounted to it. Her people stood watch on hastily created stone and moss ramparts that served as the neck of the shell.

"There she is!" A Noctave pointed to Dolli, and she waved.

Fjaar opened his mouth wider, then let Dolli step down onto his outer shell. The dungeonfolk cheered, trying to pat Dolli on the back, but their hands kept passing through her. They pulled her along through roughly crafted tunnels from the neck of the shell into the city, protected by the crystal dome.

"We did it!" someone said.

"You saved us!" another monster cried.

"For Haven!" they shouted together, ushering Dolli through to the center of town.

The elation of her people buffeted against her shock, but all she felt inside was cold. Did Taffy, Julie, Roodaulf, and the others make it, or were they consumed in the explosion? She could check her menu to see if they were in the respawn pool, but she feared what she might find. She needed to get away and find out for herself in private.

She hopped up onto an overturned cart to get above the crowd. They quieted at her presence, and she summoned her best words. "Last night, we survived a horror unlike any other trial we've been through. It was your tenacity, your willingness to put everything on the line and fight for what we still have that got us through. It was us together, as one. And so tonight, we celebrate!"

The crowd roared, jumping and cheering with a joy only felt from surviving a great battle. Dolli let it go on for a moment, then called for silence.

"Let there be a week-long festival held to honor those lost to Kelzoul's wrath. We will summon no hero to slay, we will not work except in the labor of celebrating life, and we will eat and drink enough to satiate the dead in the afterlife!"

They cheered again, every face beaming smiles at Dolli. She smiled back and addressed them a final time. "Well, we better get planning. Where's Rufus?"

"Here, Overlord," the towering Stagarth called from behind her. She turned and reached out for him. His expression shifted ever so slightly when he looked in her eyes, and she knew he could see her fear.

He took her onto his shoulder and addressed the dungeonfolk. "Let's do a bit of cleaning up, shall we? Can't be dancing with all this rubble in the way!"

He distributed a massive, dungeon-wide task for repairing the village, one that Dolli declined. She kept her breathing steady as they walked through the dispersing crowd to her cottage. She gripped his antlers tightly, the anxiety of her people's fate gnawing at her from the inside out.

All she had to do was look, and then it would be over. She could mourn or celebrate. Why was it so hard just to look?

"What's on your mind?" Rufus asked.

Dolli's stomach turned. She didn't want to tell him the shame she felt... but she trusted him above all others. He was her best counsel, and friend. "I sacrificed them to save myself," she whispered.

Rufus hummed. "Or did they sacrifice themselves to save Monster Haven?"

"I asked them to."

"But did you use your Overlord presence? Did you force them?" he asked.

They stopped at the door to the cottage. Nubiri was perched on her roost pedestal. Her gaze surveyed the village and threats outside the dome, but Dolli could tell by her tilted head that she was listening in. No matter, the village would find out the truth in time.

Dolli shook her head. "I'm not sure if I did. We were out of time, and it all happened in a blur."

Rufus opened the door. Around the table sat her officers: Greg, Brene, Boji, Julie—her arms open for an embrace. Dolli jumped from Rufus' shoulder and rushed toward her.

"I was so worried for you," Dolli said, sobbing into Julie's shoulder.

Julie patted her back with a misty hand. "Rufus returned us to the Lifewell the moment Kelzoul exploded, which ended combat for everyone."

"With you being the Overlord, I didn't have authority to return you to the Lifewell," Rufus said, taking his seat.

Greg opened the kitchen window. "We hunted the forest, messaged, called yer name, and even sent the skolfs out with yer scent—well, yer old scent."

Nubiri slipped through the opening and rested her head on the counter. "I searched Kelzoul's remainsss and the surrounding destruction for many hours."

"In short, Overlord, we were worried about *you*," Brene said.

Dolli climbed up into her seat, a peculiar feeling brewing inside her. It wasn't just the power of the Overlord commanding them to respect and obey her; they cared for her, truly. The love overwhelmed her, and she let a final blue crystal of Spark leak from her eyes. Then she wiped at it curiously. Tears? She'd never been able to cry before in this form.

"Ah, yes," Rufus said, understanding her confusion. "There seems to be much we need to discuss."

Dolli opened her menu, unprepared for the barrage of notifications. The Officer's Chat had over one hundred messages. Those she could read later, but the pop-ups that followed all demanded her attention. Dolli read them aloud to the group.

[Modulation Successful! Created Epic Dungeon Transformation – Wandering Defender]

You have used your Modulate ability against a Legendary level threat, transforming your dungeon and its play style. The following modifications have been made to the dungeon:

Dungeon is now a modified monster:

- The dungeon has Health, Spark, and all the same stats as another monster in your dungeon. Your dungeon will earn [5] stat points per level up, which you can place at your discretion or allow the dungeon to allocate. Stats affect different capabilities in the dungeon and should be read carefully. *See [Fjaar – Monster Dungeon Character Sheet] for more information.
- The dungeon can independently select its own abilities to use at will or at the command of the Overlord or Battle Commander.
- The dungeon can be modified with armor (good luck finding something big enough!).
- The dungeon cannot respawn.

Dungeon type is now Wandering Defender:

- The dungeon is now mobile. The dungeon requires Lifestream Energy to move, cast spells, and regenerate health.

Lifestream Cache:

- Lifestream Cache size for level 10 = [10,000]
- Lifestream Energy Regeneration Rate for level 10 = [159.76]/hr. *Current time to fill an emptied Lifewell: [62.6] hours*
- When the dungeon is not connected to the Lifestream, monsters must eat, drink, and sleep to recuperate along with all other necessities.
- Monsters may still be revived in the Lifewell while mobile, but the energy is depleted proportionally to the level of the monster from the Lifestream Cache. *See [Lifestream Cache Details] for more information.
- When the Lifestream Cache is emptied, the dungeon becomes stationary and cannot cast spells for [24] hours. *Disconnecting from the Lifestream applies Roaming Dungeon debuff. *See [Dungeon Abilities] for more information.*
- If the Lifestream Cache is depleted when the dungeon's Health total is 0, the dungeon will die, destroying the Overlord and setting all resident monsters free.
- The dungeon can connect to the Lifestream wherever it becomes stationary. *See [Lifestream Cache Details] for more information.

Dungeon is no longer Ascendant:

- The dungeon will not grow vertically with every level. Instead, the dungeon will grow proportionally in all directions.

=====

Next, the Lifestream connection restrictions and limitations pop-up appeared. Dolli's voice was starting to get hoarse, but she read it anyway.

[Lifestream Cache Details]

- Lifestream Cache will have reduced regeneration rates by [20%] if it is within [5] miles of another dungeon, village, or keep.
- Lifestream Cache will have reduced regeneration rates if it connects to the Lifestream in an area lacking its primary dungeon energy types by [10%] per missing energy type [Mountain | Forest | Plains].

=====

What a mouthful. Dolli was parched by the time she'd finished.

Parched…

She hadn't had a need for food or drink for over a month. Feeling the need now brought back a sense of joy in her. She solidified her form and reached for the warm tea at the center of the table.

Dolli took a moment to take in the aroma. Floral, rich, hint of herby bitterness, and a touch of sweet mountain raspberries. She took a sip, feeling the warmth, tasting the freshness of nature. It was as if all her senses had been turned back on. Perhaps it was lacking the need to eat or drink that had reduced her desire and her sensitivity to it. How strange and yet wonderful to have it all back.

"That good?" Julie asked.

"Oh, she's been missing her tea," Rufus said with a chuckle.

"I was," Dolli admitted. "And I didn't even know how much. It was easy to get caught up in battle rotations, repairs, new tasks, summon heroes, quests this and that, blood and gore and death…"

She stopped and took another drink. "Tea is life."

"If you think that's good, wait until ya taste my whiskey," Taffy's disembodied voice said from somewhere in the room.

Brene jumped to her feet, short sword pulled and ringing in her hand.

"Whoa, sorry! I didn't mean to snoop." Taffy came out of the shadows, hands raised. "It's an old habit of mine. Never trust an Overlord."

Dolli pursed her lips but motioned for Brene to stand down. "It's quite alright. Dungeonfolk are more than welcome to sit in on these officer's meetings—most of them, at least. Please, have a seat and pour yourself a cup. I guarantee it's better than any whiskey."

"So feisty! I love it." Taffy laughed and scooted a chair up next to Dolli.

When everyone was settled again, the meeting continued.

Dolli sat back in her seat. "The dungeon is changed, but I think this is to our benefit. Mobility will give us the freedom to do more of what we please, gather essential resources for improvements, and hide from any more legendary level threats."

The officers chuckled, and Dolli went on. "But there are interesting limitations that come with it. It will be a new balance we have to strike. While we're on the move, we will require food and sleep, something we are not prepared to handle. I recommend we set down for a few days, respawn all the dungeonfolk, collect some wild game and plants. We'll want to start a farming and gardening operation—"

"And we will most certainly need some of my whiskey," Taffy interjected.

The group looked at him incredulously.

Taffy held up his hands. "It's true. I'm tellin' ya, this stuff will literally make your chest hair grow."

"We will discuss space for your distillery after we've figured out logistics for the essentials," Dolli said patiently.

"I'm tellin' ya, my whiskey *is* essential," Taffy urged.

Dolli pinned him with a fiery glare.

Taffy turned red and rubbed the back of his neck. "Sure. Food first. Sorry."

The meeting went on and Taffy held his tongue for the remainder but was attentive, nonetheless. They planned farming allocations, storage, changes in respawn rotations, lodging arrangements—group barracks first, then individual homes as the dungeon grew and space allowed.

They talked until their stomachs rumbled, then agreed to reconnect to the Lifestream for the time being. The need to eat, drink, and sleep faded away and they got back to work. Morning turned to afternoon, and finally they had a workable plan of action.

Before they dispersed, Dolli pulled Greg aside. "I need you to craft something special for me—well, for a hero."

"A hero," Greg growled. "What is it?"

Dolli went to the end table next to her rocking chair, the seat of power, and pulled out an emerald portal stone. This one required an incantation, but it was one she could easily teach.

"Can you craft this into a pin, like the Officer pins? Something a hero could wear." She passed the stone to Greg.

He inspected it for a moment, then grunted. "Bet I could... not that I want to much. Who's it for?"

"The girl, Katrina. She provided necessary reinforcements in the battle. It's a teleport stone that will allow her to travel to any area I designate through this sigil," she said, holding up a bit of parchment. "Could you make something binding so she can't trade it to other heroes?"

Greg nodded. "I'll get to it soon as the necessities are managed."

"Thank you."

The group dispersed, save for Rufus and Taffy. Rufus looked as though he needed a moment of her time alone.

"If you wait for me at the X I can help find a spot to get your distillery started," Dolli said to Taffy. "I think near my alchemy lab would be optimal. We can enlarge the Spark shield around both buildings to protect the surrounding businesses from… the undesirable side effects of brewing."

Taffy snapped both fingers and pointed to Dolli, saying, "Sounds like a plan," then left them alone.

When the cottage was clear, Rufus spoke. "Is it wise to give a hero unlimited access to Haven?"

"It's relatively safe. We can easily kill her in her current state, but she's useful in a pinch and knows how to get alchemy materials. I need someone who can go into towns and copy spells from the local apothecaries."

Rufus scowled. "What's this really about?"

Dolli was quiet for a moment.

Too long a moment.

Rufus hummed knowingly. "So, you're back on the old quest."

"You more than anyone should understand why I want to do it."

"I thought you liked this hero?"

Dolli nodded. "She's kinder than most. I think coming to understand their perspective has helped me not to hate them so much, but that doesn't mean I want them here anymore. I need to build trust so she'll tell me more about her world, and lead us to answers."

The room fell to silence, and Rufus poured himself a bit of tea from the cool kettle.

"Am I wrong?" she asked.

Rufus shook his head. "I couldn't say."

Dolli crossed her arms and balked. "You wanted to murder them so bad you were willing to be transformed into a dungeon monster."

He hummed, nodding. "And I've done a fair amount of hero murdering."

"For your sons' sake, Rufus, we must do this. For the sake of all Hafheim's sons and daughters, we can't allow the heroes to come here anymore."

"You think giving this Katrina unlimited access to Monster Haven will get you closer to that end?" Rufus asked.

"I think she has access to ancient cities with ancient texts from the Shamans of Old, and I know if I ask, she'll get them for us."

"She figured out what the potion was for with relative ease. Are you certain you'll be able to build the necessary trust for such an ask in the shadow of a lie?"

Dolli sucked down a deep breath. "I have to try."

Rufus dipped his head. "And I'll support that decision when the time comes."

"Because you believe in it, or because I'm your Overlord?"

Rufus sighed and rested a hand on Dolli's shoulder. "Because I trust that no matter what happens, you'll fight for us, and we'll find a way to get through anything."

He set his teacup down and turned for the door.

"Am I making a mistake?"

Rufus paused, then shrugged. "Many choices still lie ahead of us. Who knows what the next one might bring?"

"What is it with all the philosophical questions today?"

"I'm feeling thoughtful after facing my death," Rufus said, tapping his chin in mock thought.

"I hope my choices don't bring us to ruin... again," Dolli said, the words heavy in her heart.

Rufus chuckled and picked up a bit of debris from the dusty floor. "What's a bit of ruin in the face of Monster Haven's tenacity?"

Dolli smiled. "Nothin' at all."

Rufus opened the door and headed out into the breezy autumn afternoon. All she wanted for her people was peace and prosperity. She'd go to great lengths to get it for them. After what they'd all been through, they deserved it. She knew it could be done, and now she had the means to figure it out.

It was time to end the heroes' invasion of Hafheim and close the realm portals for good.

THE END
Revenging Dungeon
Monster Haven Book 2

ROAMING DUNGEON

J.D. ASTRA

MONSTER HAVEN BOOK THREE

THE ADVENTURE CONTINUES...

... in *Roaming Dungeon (Monster Haven Book 3)*.

'Tis the season to be jolly... assuming jolly means murderous.

Dollitrice Grandmeir never thought her village would turn into a dungeon, or that she'd battle a Kaiju Overlord with the help of her giant Tortoise. Now she's got an all-new weirdness on her radar. The Twelve Days of Crisismas are coming, and without a special brew of Eggnog, Taffy and the Ex-Mas Posse will transform into horrific Grumpus monsters, annihilating Dolli's dungeon from the inside out.

That special brew—Egg Noggin-Fogger—is just what the Neckbeards ordered. The guild of heroes raids Monster Haven relentlessly to get their hands on the whiskey blend, pushing back the Posse's production and putting the whole brew at risk. If they can't get a few days of peace and quiet, they'll have no choice but to flee Monster Haven to prepare for the horrific transformation.

Dolli must take her dungeon on the road to avoid the raids, all while searching for her own game ender: Sherkahn's Shillelagh, a tool of the heroes' own making that has the power to close the portals to her world once and for all. Can they evade the Neckbeards long enough to complete the brew, or will Dolli have to send her merry elf additions into the wilds to protect her dungeon and finish the quest for the staff?

BOOKS AND REVIEWS

If you loved *Revenging Dungeon* and would like stay in the loop about the latest book releases, deals, and giveaways, be sure to subscribe to the Shadow Alley Press Mailing List.

www.ShadowAlleyPress.com

Sign up now and get a free copy of our bestselling anthology, Viridian Gate Online: Side Quests! Your email address will never be shared and you can unsubscribe at any time.

Word-of-mouth and book reviews are beyond helpful for the success of any writer, so please consider leaving a rating or a short, honest review on Amazon—just a couple of lines about your overall reading experience. Thank you in advance!

You can also connect with us on our Facebook Page where we do even more giveaways: facebook.com/shadowalleypress

BOOKS BY SHADOW ALLEY PRESS

ENTER THE SHADOW ALLEY LIBRARY to take a peek at all of our amazing Gamelit, Fantasy, and Science Fiction books! Viridian Gate Online, Rogue Dungeon, Snake's Life, Dungeon Heart, Path of the Thunderbird, School of Swords and Serpents, the FiveFold Universe, and so many more... Your next favorite book is waiting for you inside!

A WORD FROM (JESS) J.D. ASTRA!

Henlo there my dudes! I hope you enjoyed the read, and really look forward to seeing your thoughts online! Come hang out in my discord server:

https://discord.gg/ZRSSvgRh6k

Not a fan of Discord? Follow me on Facebook for memes and updates here:

https://www.facebook.com/theastralscribe

If Facebook isn't your thing, you can sign up for my mailing list for a free novella set in the Bastion Academy series, and get monthly updates here:

http://subscribe.astralscribe.com/bastionsubs

If you're looking to support me (<3 thank you!) and get super exclusive access to early chapters, arts, special updates, and more, you can find me on Patreon here:

https://www.patreon.com/jdastra

Here's some of those awesome Patrons, my Friendly Townsfolk+:

Tyler O. | eden H. | Janet S. | Joseph O. | Ken R. | Laura L. | Remy J. | Ray Allen | Daniel M.

STILL not seeing your jam? These things receive less love, but...

I have a website: www.astralscribe.com

You can email me directly: contact@astralscribe.com

TikTok: @jd_astra

ABOUT THE AUTHOR

About me... I'm a baller. Keyboard crawler. 20 inch display, on my ink scrawler. Holler. Getting flayed tonight, all my characters getting splayed tonight!

In my spare time I love to cook, hike, play video games, and spend quality time with my people.

Three questions people never ask me are; how do I look at myself in the mirror, what's in the box, and what does it take to build a story with likable characters in an interesting setting with important goals?

The answer to the last is determination, dedication, and sacrifice. I've been working at being a writer since before I could string more than two sentences together, and it never gets easier, but it does get better.

I'm surrounded by people who love and support me, which is the most amazing gift the universe could ever give. I will never give up, never surrender, and hopefully, keep on entertaining for the rest of my life.